ADDRESS UNKNOWN

Address
Unknown

by

MALCOLM HUTTON

St. Martin's Press
New York

Copyright © 1981 by Malcolm Hutton
For information, write: St. Martin's Press,
175 Fifth Avenue, New York, N.Y. 10010
Manufactured in the United States of America

Library of Congress Cataloging in Publication Data

Hutton, Malcolm.
    Address unknown.

    I.   Title.
PR6058.U8598A64   1981   823'.914   81-5762
ISBN 0-312-00427-3   AACR2

One

Mr Godfrey was depressed—more depressed than he'd been at any other time in his life. And he felt old, very old. His thin frame leaned into the wind and his white hair blew untidily over his forehead as he made his way across Putney Bridge to the underground station. The rain was spattering his spectacles and every now and then he stopped and wiped them with a handkerchief.

He hadn't any particular destination in mind. He simply wanted to go somewhere to think. If the weather hadn't been so wretched he'd have sat in the park down by the river and thought over his troubles there. He couldn't meditate at home, not with Mrs Godfrey about the place. She'd be hoovering around him in the sitting-room or she'd decide to do the washing. The washing-machine made a din like a jet taking off and vibrated the whole ground floor of their small semi. Besides, if he returned home he'd have to tell her about the awful thing that had happened to him today. He couldn't do that. When he'd left home that morning she believed he was on his way to his old office to fill in some forms about his pension. She didn't understand that nothing would induce him to go there again.

Thirty-seven years he'd worked for the Council. *Thirty-seven years.* Then, two months ago, with no warning, they'd told him he was to be made redundant. Mrs Godfrey said he should be thankful that the redundancy terms were as good as they were, as though money made up for everything. Of course, he'd been due to retire in a few years anyway, but that would have been different. He could have planned for that. There would have been a collection. A retirement party. Farewell speeches. He would have departed with dignity. Instead, he'd had to slink away. Discarded. *Redundant.* The very word sounded shameful. He was useless. Unwanted.

He reached the underground station, dried his glasses once more and studied the map of London's Underground on the wall beside the ticket office. Where should he book to? A long, long time ago—but he could recall it like yesterday—he'd travelled to school on the Tube. Happy times those had been. Why, as you grew older, was it so easy to remember childhood, when you could hardly recall what happened last year, or even last week?

Mr Godfrey peered undecidedly at the map, trying to make up his mind. Where could he sit undisturbed while he thought out what to do? Like changing to a different channel on television, his mind slipped away to his schooldays again. Often when he'd been at a loose end or didn't want to go home for a while, he used to ride round and round the Inner Circle. That's what he'd do. He'd go for a ride on the Circle Line. Any station would do.

'Return to Barbican, please,' he told the booking-clerk.

It was late evening and the rush-hour on the Underground was over. Trains travelling outwards from the central area carried only a handful of passengers.

On the Jubilee Line, Old Charlie settled into his seat, splayed out his legs and closed his eyes. The bottle of wine mixed with methylated spirits bulged comfortingly against his side in the pocket of his stained raincoat. He'd

6

have a zizz as far as Wembley Park, nip off there and slip across to the up platform. The large electric panel heater in the waiting-room there gave out a satisfying warmth and he could snuggle into a corner, swigging from his bottle until it was time to take the last train back into town.

Drifting peacefully, his stubbled chin sunk into his chest, Charlie marked the coming and going of each station by the noise of the automatic doors and the draughts of cold air as they opened and closed. At Neasden a sudden clatter of boots into the carriage broke the pattern and he registered the fact with a return to a higher level of consciousness.

There were three of them, with shaved heads and vacant, grinning faces. They wore straight jeans and black, zip-jackets. Two of them plomped into the seats either side of him with deliberate clumsiness so that he was bounced up in his own seat. The third stood over him, planting his booted feet between Charlie's open legs and nonchalantly reaching up to grasp two of the hanging knobs suspended from the carriage roof.

Skinheads. Wide awake now, Old Charlie looked fearfully up and down the carriage. The only other occupants were two Asians at the far end who were carefully ignoring him. He tried to rise so as to change his seat but from each side a vice-like grip clamped his bony wrists to the arm-rests and held him down. He raised his head and gazed into the bleak, mindless eyes.

'What d'yer want?'

'Now, what d'ya think we want, you scabby old goat?'

'I ain't got a penny. Honest to God I ain't.'

'He ain't got a penny,' they told one another, bellowing with laughter.

'Turn him up and shake him about,' said one.

'Put him down and trample his nuts,' said another.

The Skinhead standing over him casually unzipped his

jacket to display the length of chain round his waist. He thrust his pelvis forward aggressively.

'Next stop we's taking you up the end of the platform for a chit-chat. Sort things out. Know what I mean? You old winos always have lolly stashed away somewhere.'

'Well, *I* ain't,' Charlie whined. He trembled at the mean look in the youth's face and his addled brain hunted desperately for a means of salvation. A crafty expression came into his eyes.

'I've got nothing. Straight up. I know where there *is* some cash though.' Eager to convince them and save himself he let his imagination speak. 'There's so much I reckon it must be hot!'

'Yeh, where?'

'Baker Street—down in the new building work. I'll show you boys the place,' said Charlie eagerly. Anything to get back to the centre of London where there were more people. Out here he hadn't a chance. These louts would beat him up just for the pleasure it gave them. He was too old to stand a beating, but they wouldn't care.

For a few agonising moments he watched his fate being decided. Then the Skinhead standing over him said:

'You do that. You show us.' He reached down and seized the neck of Charlie's shirt. 'If you're having us on, you old git, you'll get a going over like you won't never forget.'

Mr Godfrey hadn't travelled the Underground much in recent years. His journey to and from work had been by bus. Occasionally he and Mrs Godfrey had made an evening trip to the West End; and once or twice they'd taken the Central Line to Gants Hill to visit Mrs Godfrey's sister. He was shocked to discover how much London's Underground had changed. The trains were packed even when the rush-hour had ended; and most of the passengers seemed to be foreign: Chinese-looking youths of one sort or another, Iranians, Arabs, all sorts and mixtures of nationalities. Not many of the passengers seemed to be British or even European. Perhaps it was different at other times of day.

The carriages were dirty, the floors covered with litter and the windows grimy. As his train passed through Earls Court he was appalled at the defacement of the advertisement hoardings. Most of the scrawling was incomprehensible because it was in Arabic—or it could have been Persian or Hebrew for all he knew. It had come to something, thought Mr Godfrey, when a man couldn't understand the graffiti in his own capital City. He stared sadly at the ripped seats, the trails of paint across the carriage roof and wondered what kind of person did these things. Kids, he supposed; or adults with the minds of children.

At Gloucester Road he'd left the Putney train to change to the Circle Line and found himself faced with a decision. Which way round should he go? Should he go eastwards, anti-clockwise, or cross the platform to take a westbound train and travel clockwise. Surely it came to the same thing? He'd dithered, unable to make up his mind. In the end he'd pulled a coin from his pocket. Heads, eastwards. Tails, westward. He'd opened his palm and looked down. It was heads.

He had journeyed round and round the Circle; or, to be more exact, he'd completed the circuit three times. It was now late evening and he was no nearer to making up his mind what to do than when he'd started and he still didn't feel like returning home to face Mrs Godfrey. Also he was plagued by another problem. He was finding it quite difficult to recall the day's events. The harder he tried the more his mind seemed to close up. Another time he'd find two pictures occupying his mind at once, which was very confusing. Probably it was because he was tired and hadn't eaten since breakfast.

Three times on the journey to Baker Street Old Charlie had thought of doing a bolt; but two of the Skinheads flanked him all the time. If they hadn't allowed him an occasional pull at his bottle, his legs would have given way in fright. It wasn't that he had nothing to show them —he hadn't been that crazy. He simply wasn't sure there really was any money hidden where he'd said. His brain wasn't too clear these days. If he'd made a mistake they'd smash him to pieces.

He'd noticed the haversacks and bedrolls several evenings running. They were hidden in a disused passage in the labyrinth of alleyways and old passages behind the building work for the Baker Street extension. Often he'd lie around there himself in the early evening. Sometimes he returned there for his night's kip. The gear was never there overnight. Earlier this evening he'd seen a youth kneeling at one of the haversacks and he'd swear he'd counted some notes and stuffed them in one of the compartments. The boy hadn't seen him lying there in the gloom amid the litter and rubbish. Charlie hadn't touched the gear, of course. Fallen on hard times he might be, but he wasn't a thief. But now he wasn't sure if he'd been dreaming—he wasn't always clear what was real and what were dreams any more.

Charlie led the Skinheads behind the scaffolding and into the complex of passages beyond, some dark, some well-lit by lamps hooked into the station circuits. He knew the area like his own hand. He almost collapsed with relief to find the bright blue sleeping-bags just where he'd thought they were. As the Skins dragged them out and opened them, becoming absorbed in their search, Charlie decided to take his chance. He took to his heels, scurrying down another passage.

They caught him at the first bend. Gleefully, as though this was just the excuse they'd been waiting for, they laid into him with their fists. His low whimpers were lost in the thud of blows.

Along the same route as Charlie had brought the Skinheads, three children now approached the hiding-place: a ginger-haired boy of fifteen or sixteen and two girls. The smaller girl, a tubby little thing in a grey, furry coat, had straight black hair, cut short. The older girl, in blue jeans, was tall and slim with long, fair hair that reached to her shoulders. The trio came to the scattered sleeping-bags and haversacks and regarded them with dismay. From the adjacent passage they heard the noise of shouts and scuffles as Charlie fell to the ground and the Skins substituted feet for fists and began booting him. Quickly the children repacked their possessions. The boy felt in the pocket of one of the haversacks.

'The money's gone, Sis!'

'Never mind, let's get away from here,' she said urgently.

They hoisted the bedrolls and two of the haversacks on to their shoulders. The small girl shouldered the other haversack and they started back the way they had come. The boy waved the two girls on and took a few steps along the passageway from where the sounds were coming. He rounded a bend and nearly collided with the Skinheads who were returning to resume their search.

The leader recognised the haversack on the boy's shoulders.

'Drop that!' he ordered.

The boy did a fast about-turn and ran. The Skinheads charged after him but he was fit and nimble and despite his burden he reached the end of the passage well ahead of them. The older of the two girls was waiting beside two stacks of bricks which almost blocked the way out leaving only a narrow space between them.

'Hurry, Martin!' she cried.

As he squeezed through she gave a vigorous push to the top of the stacks and the bricks tumbled down, filling

11

the opening and cascading across the Skinheads' paths. Cursing and swearing they stumbled about trying to get through. The girl picked up a brick and hurled it at the gang. It caught the leader, Butch Fearon, in the face and sliced open his cheek. He howled with rage, clapping a hand to his injured face. The boy and girl retreated swiftly. They emerged from behind the building work, hurried to the escalators and raced down them to where the little girl waited at the foot. Together they ran to the Bakerloo Line where a train was rumbling into the plat-form.

The Skinheads crashed their way over the bricks and stampeded down the escalator after them. They burst on to the platform as the train doors were closing. Three frightened faces stared out from the safety of the carriage. The Skinheads kicked and banged on the doors, yelling and whistling at the guard to open them but he ignored them and the train moved off. They ran along the plat-form making obscene signs and mouthing threats to the youngsters inside until the train disappeared into the tunnel.

An hour later Old Charlie partially regained conscious-ness. Painfully he dragged himself an inch at a time along the rubble-strewn floor, appealing weakly to every Deity he knew. 'Oh, God . . . Jesus . . . Holy Mother . . . help me.'

An age later he pushed aside some planking and fell out into a tiled passageway between the platforms. A passing woman screamed and drew away from the blood-stained thing gibbering at her feet. She hurried on. 'One of those dreadful meths men,' she told her husband later. 'He nearly touched my ankle.'

Some late-night passengers stopped and looked down uncertainly. A girl in a white evening gown stepped forward. Hitching up the tight skirt she stooped beside Old Charlie, displaying a great deal of leg to the annoyance of the man who was with her.

'Come away, he's only some old drunk.'

The girl looked up. 'Call an ambulance,' she said curtly, 'he's very badly hurt.'

A long way from Baker Street—far out on the Upminster Line in fact—Mr Godfrey was sleeping in the kind of warm waiting-room that would have delighted poor Old Charlie. The only decision Mr Godfrey had come to was that he wouldn't go home. When the last train had departed he'd hidden himself while the porter went his rounds and closed the station. Then he'd settled down in the waiting-room to spend the night.

Two

Mr Godfrey did not spend a comfortable night. Not only was the bench seat in the waiting-room very hard but the mental block, or whatever it was, that had prevented him recalling yesterday's events clearly, now seemed to be operating in reverse and his thoughts were filled with yesterday's unpleasantness. He was a very respectable, upright citizen, a Town Hall employee—ex-employee, he reminded himself sourly—and nothing like that had happened to him before.

That morning he'd set out with no particular purpose in mind and he'd wandered along the High Street gazing aimlessly into the shop windows. What he'd told his wife about calling at his old office had been simply an excuse. The truth was that he didn't know what to do with himself. Over the years he'd become conditioned to going to the office each day and to spending his evenings and week-ends watching television or tending his small garden. He had no idea of how to cope with being home all day.

'You must occupy your time,' Mrs Godfrey had said sharply when he'd tried to discuss the future with her the evening before. 'Find yourself a nice little hobby. One that's not messy,' she added.

'I want to do something *useful*!'

'Useful?' She'd given him that look of hers—full of doubt. It always killed any spark of initiative in him. After a pause, to make sure her doubts had registered with him: 'What about stamp collecting? You used to like stamps.' That had been the end of the discussion.

Along the High Street he'd entered one of the stores. He supposed he'd spent some time looking around. Then he must have left. The store detective who grabbed him on the pavement—rudely gripping his arm as though he were a criminal—had been cold and cynical.

'Save your breath, I've heard the story a hundred times before,' he sneered when Mr Godfrey protested that he hadn't intended to take the electric razor without paying for it.

With alarming speed Mr Godfrey found himself first in the Manager's office and then at the police station making a statement. *Theft*. That's what he was to be charged with. And what worried him almost as much as the offence was the fact that he couldn't understand how on earth it had happened. Was he losing his faculties? He remembered picking up one of the electric razors from the counter. There had been a sensual feel to its sleek, black body as he fitted it neatly to the grip of his fingers. He'd shaved with soap and water and a safety razor ever since he'd begun shaving regularly at the age of seventeen. It was hard to break old habits. Should he make the change?

'Times change, Godfrey!' That's what the Head of Section had said when he informed Mr Godfrey that he was being made redundant. 'We must change with the times. Even *I* have had to change.' What he meant, of course, was that *his* change would be to new duties in another part of the office. It was Mr Godfrey who had suffered the real change. He was out of a job.

His thoughts had still been on the office when the store detective challenged him outside in the street. The razor was in his pocket then. Had he meant to steal it? He honestly didn't know and he resented the way the detective and the police thought he was putting on an act.

'I really can't explain how it happened,' he said. 'I'm not short of money. I can easily pay for the article.'

'Your sort usually can,' said the policeman nastily. 'That isn't the point. You took it without paying.'

'But I didn't *mean* to.'

'Yes, well you can explain that in Court.'

Afterwards Mr Godfrey returned to the store. He felt confused and aggrieved. Perversely, he'd decided he *would* have an electric razor. What's more, he'd have the very one they said he'd tried to steal. The store detective appeared beside him.

'What are you doing back here?' he asked unpleasantly.

'I intend to purchase the item you refused to allow me to pay for earlier.'

The man's eyes glinted. He was short and heavily-built. One hand fiddled with a waistcoat button. The other moved restlessly deep in the pocket of his baggy trousers.

'Not that one, you can't. Not that particular one. Oh dear no.' He rocked on his heels. 'That's *evidence*.'

'Very well, then, I shall choose one exactly the same.'

'Make sure you take it to the cashier. With the money!' Both hands were in his pockets now, digging into the crutch area of his trousers. As he moved away he added, without lowering his voice, 'I *hate* thieves.' Angrily, Mr Godfrey had made the purchase and hurried from the store.

He recalled the scene vividly as he awoke in the station waiting-room and it made him flush with shame. To be spoken to in that way—and by a man like that! He'd wanted to crawl away and die. No, that was foolish, that was just a saying. Mr Godfrey had dreamed about death and about funerals lately. Was it an omen? He didn't *wish* for death but he couldn't say he would actually *object* to dying. Which would be his path to the grave? Cancer? A coronary? And how long had he got? Ah, there was the rub. No one ever knew, of course. What he really wanted, he thought, was for something interesting to happen to him. Something that would change his life. *Give me back the will to live!* he felt like shouting, *Give me something to live for.*

He kept out of sight until the first train in the morning arrived and then slipped aboard as the doors were closing. In spite of his depression he was ravenously hungry and he changed at Whitechapel and caught a train to Liverpool Street where he was pretty certain there was a cafe. A wash and shave freshened him up; and he felt a wry pleasure at using the electric battery-shaver that had caused such trouble yesterday. By the time he'd finished a good meal he was almost cheerful. What should he do today? Take a trip into the country? He sat thoughtfully sipping his third cup of tea, searching his memory. Eastcote. That was in the country—or it used to be. The name struck a chord. Old memories of his schooldays drifted into his mind. He tried to remember a name. A nickname. She'd had a funny nickname. *Chick*. Probably a pet name given to her by her father. He couldn't remember her actual first name—if he'd ever known it—and he couldn't for the moment think of her surname. She'd lived at Eastcote. They'd walked across the fields together, schoolgirl, schoolboy. Yes, he'd travel out to Eastcote and see what it was like today.

He went down to the Central Line en route for Oxford Circus, Baker Street and the Metropolitan Line.

Mr Godfrey was still trying to recall the surname of his schoolgirl sweetheart when the train stopped at Tottenham Court Road. Among the passengers surging into the carriage were two girls, one of them, aged about thirteen, with a solemn, oval face and blonde, shoulder-length hair. Mr Godfrey realised that she looked a little like

Chick. Ah! He had the surname now. *Courtney.* Chick Courtney.

This girl was wearing jeans. Chick Courtney had never worn jeans, of course. They were unheard of in those days. The War had changed all that. Even Mrs Godfrey had worn trousers in the WAAF when he met her. Come to think of it she'd been wearing them most of the time ever since. She seemed to prefer trousers to dresses and skirts.

The other girl was much younger—a plump child in a pale-blue dress with straight, jet-black hair and a round face. Her eyes slanted slightly giving her a rather oriental look. Her head was lost in the stand-up collar of her short, furry coat. Both girls clung to one of the upright supports as the train lurched along.

All at once there was a clatter and the communicating door at the end of the carriage opened. The girls reared their heads like startled ponies as two ticket inspectors in peaked caps stepped in from the next carriage.

'Tickets please! Have your tickets ready!'

The men moved through the carriage checking tickets. There was an urgent whispered consultation between the two girls.

'Your ticket, please.' The first man reached the older girl and loomed over her.

She stared up at him blankly. 'Lost it,' she said.

'I see,' said the inspector. His expression reminded Mr Godfrey of the store detective earlier that morning. He'd had that satisfied look—as though he were pleased to have caught someone out. The man dragged a receipt book from his pocket, licked his thumb and turned over a page.

'Where'd you get on?' he asked, pencil poised.

There was a change in the noise from the tunnel as the train neared the next station.

'Can't remember,' said the girl. Mr Godfry noticed that

18

she was edging the other girl towards the doors.

The man flushed angrily. 'Right!' He put away the receipt book and pulled out a notebook. 'Name and address!' he snapped.

The train slowed rapidly and shuddered to a halt at Oxford Circus. Mr Godfrey rose to his feet. This was where he changed to the Bakerloo Line.

'What's your name and where d'you live?' the man demanded of the girl impatiently. The smaller one's eyes, watching her companion's face, were like saucers.

The doors started to slide apart. Suddenly the older girl lashed out with her foot, hacking the ticket inspector on the shins.

'*SPLIT!*' she screeched.

Both girls bolted on to the platform. One ran left, the other right. With a roar of pain and anger the inspector half-hopped, half-leapt out after them, scattering the people waiting to enter. His colleague jumped out after him. Mr Godfrey pushed his way through the incoming passengers.

On the platform the two men were hesitating, uncertain which girl to follow and losing vital seconds. Then, presumably deciding that she'd be the easier to catch, they gave chase to the smaller girl who was bobbing and weaving along the crowded platform towards the WAY OUT sign. In the other direction Mr Godfrey saw the blonde girl disappearing into the passage leading to the Victoria Line. He turned and followed the ticket inspectors, although at a more leisurely pace, because this was also the way to the Bakerloo Line. At the foot of the escalators he paused to watch the continuing chase.

The girl scuttled up an escalator hotly pursued by the two men. Being bulkier they had to push their way past people and they began to lose ground. However, the end seemed inevitable to Mr Godfrey; the girl would be trapped by the ticket collector at the exit barrier. At the top of the escalator, with a flash of white knicker under the short dress as she skipped off the end, she went from his view.

The two men were nearing the top themselves. Then, on the 'Down' escalator, Mr Godfrey glimpsed the blue dress again and realised, with amusement, that the girl had doubled across and was on the way down again. He saw her crouching behind the skirts of a fat, black woman. The ticket inspectors were now out of sight, no doubt conferring with the collector at the barrier, checking if he'd let the girl through.

She came off the foot of the escalator by Mr Godfrey, panting like a little hunted animal. With a quick backward glance to make sure she hadn't been spotted, she ran down the stairs leading to the Bakerloo Line. Mr Godfrey followed sedately. Although he couldn't approve of bilking London Transport, he was glad she'd escaped. As he stepped on to the northbound platform a train was already disgorging its load and he only had time to jump inside before the doors closed. The little girl had entered the same carriage ahead of him and he saw her flop, gasping, into an empty seat. He wondered if she realised that her companion had gone to the Victoria Line. He sat down opposite to her. Puffing and blowing she fanned her face with her hand. She struggled out of her coat and laid it on the seat beside her. Then she lifted each leg in turn and straightened her white, wrinkled socks. When she seemed to have settled Mr Godfrey bent forward.

'Excuse me, but your friend—the girl you were with —she went through to the Victoria Line, you know.'

The girl stared at him, unwinking, and he felt suddenly foolish. Perhaps she didn't speak English. After all, he'd only heard the other girl shout one word at her. As he was about to speak again she leaned towards him and said in a rush, her eyes blinking rapidly:

'She's not a friend. That's Sarah, me sister—and I'm not supposed to talk to strange men.' Her mouth closed firmly and she averted her head to gaze out of the window at the side of the tunnel racing past.

'Yes, I understand,' murmured Mr Godfrey. He thought she could have shown more appreciation of the information he'd given her. She was very young and he was only trying to reunite her with her sister. He persevered.

'But shouldn't you go back and find her? She might be waiting for you there.'

She continued to stare out of the window and answered him without turning her head.

'No, she'll be going out Cockfosters way. Sarah likes the Piccadilly Line. Me, I like the Bakerloo. It smells nicer and 'sides, you see more country out near Watford. 'It's OK,' she went on, 'we always meet up in the cafe at Liverpool Street at five o'clock.'

None of this made much sense to Mr Godfrey. However, she seemed to have forgotten the rule about talking to strangers.

'What's your name?' he asked.

'Elsie.'

'How old are you, Elsie?'

'I'm nine.' She drew one leg up to the seat and began picking a scab on her knee at the same time watching him from the corner of her eyes.

'And where do you live?'

She put her feet down again and waggled her feet about, studying her shoe.

'Where do you live?' he repeated. He thought he should at least make sure that she knew where she was going and was on the right route. The train was coming into Regents Park station.

'Questions, questions,' she muttered. 'What you asking me all these questions for?'

'I was only trying to make sure you're all right—you're

rather young to be wandering about on the Tube alone.'
The train halted and the doors opened.

She timed it perfectly. At the instant of the hiss of air as
the doors were about to close, she leapt from her seat and
catapulted herself towards them. Her small, round body
ejected neatly through the closing gap with nothing to
spare.

On the platform she made a face at him through the
window. 'We live on the Tube, silly!' she yelled, giving a
jaunty wave as the train moved away.

'What nonsense!' Mr Godfrey snorted. Then he noticed
the cheap, nylon-fur coat still lying on the seat. He picked
it up and looked in the worn lining for a name and
address tag. There wasn't one. He supposed he'd have to
hand the coat in as lost property.

The train rattled into Baker Street and he alighted,
holding the furry garment self-consciously over his arm.
The draft of cold air as he ascended to the Metropolitan
Line above ground reminded him that it was winter.
She'd be cold without a coat this weather and somehow
he didn't think she'd have another one. It might be days
before she recovered it from Lost Property, even assuming
she went there. He searched in the pockets for a purse or
wallet that might show an address or a telephone number.
There was a screwed-up tissue and several chocolate
wrappers in one pocket. In the other he found a small, fat
purse in the shape of a mouse, the zip-fastener running
along its back. The purse was crammed with coins, mostly
ten-pence pieces, but there was nothing to indicate where
the girl lived.

*We always meet up in the cafe at Liverpool Street at five
o'clock*. That was what she had said. Well, perhaps after
he'd been out to Eastcote, and maybe had a spot of lunch,
he would return to Liverpool Street and see if she showed
up. That seemed a helpful idea and, anway, he had
nothing better to do.

Three

Butch Fearon scanned the lunchtime edition of the papers, his bent head seeming a grey, mud-colour because of the closely-cropped hair. He was looking for a mention of the old man they'd beaten up last night because he knew, better than the other two, how savagely he'd put the boot in. He was half-expecting the report in the paper but not—his eyes widened in alarm—not that the old fool had *died*. He read the paragraph again. *Baker Street . . . late yesterday evening . . . an elderly man . . . .* It was the old wino right enough.

Butch felt no remorse, only a worry about himself. He chewed his lips in concentration. Best if Sid and Terry didn't know about this. They'd only get in a sweat. No one would connect the three of them with that lump of fuddled human rubbish. The ginger-haired boy and those girls had seen nothing. Besides, kids didn't read newspapers.

When Sid and Terry joined him for their regular midday drink Butch directed their thoughts to money. 'We gotta find them kids' gear again,' he told them, 'an' nick the rest of their loot.'

Sid said doubtfully: 'P'raps that old sod's brain was just burned away with the meths and he didn't know what he was saying.'

23

'He was right though, wasn't he? There was thirty oncers in them two fag packets we took out the haversack and there was another twenty packets at least. There must be three or four hundred quid all told.'

'Maybe the others are just full of smokes,' Terry suggested.

'Don't be daft! Even if the kid smoked he wouldn't cart *twenty* packets of fags around with him now would he?'

'But where would they get that kind of bread?'

'Maybe they found it, or maybe their dear old dad did a job and they're hiding it for him. How the Hell should I know? Point is Terry, we gotta find them and see. The old dosser said they were always around down there—he reckoned they'd nowhere else to go.' Butch gently touched the open wound on his cheek. ''Sides, I want words with that blonde bit.'

'Think you'll scar, Butch?' Sid asked.

'Yeh, reckon I will.' His eyes shone balefully. 'And she's gonna get a good fingering for that!'

'Where do we look though?' Terry asked. 'There's hundreds of stations.'

'We'll only do the centre. We'll split up and do a Line each and we'll meet up every hour on the platform at the 'Dilly.'

It had stopped raining. Mr Godfrey sat on Eastcote station lost in thought. The pleasant, clean smell in the air after the rain evoked memories of his schooldays: clear, sharp images of himself and Chick Courtney walking hand in hand through the woods after rain. Drops falling from the trees, the scent of wet grass.

Their schools were close together near Shepherd's Bush. They both travelled to school by electric train, but on different lines. He lived at Ealing and she lived at Eastcote. Chick was his first schoolgirl sweetheart and the young Godfrey was very much in love. For the whole of a

24

summer term he journeyed out to Eastcote with her every day after school and then travelled all the way home again to Ealing. His mother thought he stayed behind at school to play chess.

The purpose of this pilgrimage was to be alone with Chick at the end of her journey. In those days the latest extension of the Piccadilly Line reached only to Rayners Lane. Here Chick Courtney had to change trains and travel the Old Metropolitan Line to Eastcote.

Unlike the Piccadilly Line trains, the old brown trains of the Metropolitan Line had separate, five-a-side compartments. He and Chick would find an empty compartment —not difficult at that time of day—and sit opposite each other, their knees touching, holding hands. Chick would throw off her school hat and down would tumble her long, golden hair. It was the signal for him to lean forward and kiss her. He remembered how furiously she used to blush, the red of her cheeks as bright as strawberry stains, and how she never failed to meet his lips eagerly with her own.

Had he really gone all that way, day after day, for a few schoolgirl kisses? Mr Godfrey sighed, happy in his memories. He had indeed. He could see her now . . . summer uniform of blue and white gingham . . . straw boater crammed down on her head so that it pushed out her hair to frame her face. He'd thought she was the most lovely creature he'd ever seen.

Mr Godfrey saw the bright blue dress shining like a beacon through the window of the buffet bar at Liverpool Street even before he entered. She was perched on one of the high stools at the counter, her feet barely reaching the crossbar. She was gripping a glass of milkshake with both hands while she sucked energetically at the two straws dipped into it.

He approached her from behind. 'Hullo, Elsie,' he said in her ear. 'Here's your coat.'

She choked on the straws, spat them out and swivelled round. Her face lit up.

'You've got me coat! Oh, tah! I thought I'd lost it for good.'

He laid it on the stool next to her. 'There's a purse full of money in the pocket.'

'Yeh, that's me finders-keepers money. Tah for bringing it back.' She turned to the counter and clamped her mouth over the straws again.

'Finders-keepers money? What's that?' Mr Godfrey spoke above the bubbling noises Elsie was making as she came to the bottom of the glass. Reluctantly, she released the straws from her mouth. The ends sagged limply over the rim like blades of chewed grass.

'It's from the fags and sweet machines. I try 'em all . . . on every station. Sometimes there's a coin left in the slot and sometimes a drawer opens and I get a bar of choccy or a packet of fags. I give the fags to Martin.'

'Martin? Who's Martin?'

'Me brother. He lives down the Tube with Sarah an' me.'

There she went again with that nonsense tale. He said jokingly:

'I see. You have a sister, Sarah—the girl you were with this morning—and you have a brother called Martin and—' he drew it out slowly '—you-all-live-on-the-Tube?'

'Yeh, that's right.' She sounded bored. 'An' I'm getting fed-up with it.'

Perhaps she was batty. He'd better not leave her until the sister arrived.

She looked longingly at the empty glass and the mutilated straws. 'I'm still thirsty,' she said. He ignored the hint. 'What's your name?' she asked, changing direction like a grasshopper.

26

'Godfrey.'

'I knew a Godfrey at school. He used to—'

'That's not my first name. I'm called Arnold. Arnold Godfrey.'

'*Arnold!*' To his annoyance, she giggled. 'What a funny name.'

She lifted her knees up but her feet slipped. She tried again and hugged them under her chin with her arms.

'You bin riding round on the trains all day?' Her tone implied that it would be quite normal.

'Yes, I have, as a matter of fact.'

Thoughtfully, she rubbed her chin on the hem of her dress. Her voice dropped confidentially. 'You on the run?'

He laughed aloud. Then he thought about it. He was, in a way.

'Well, yes. Sort of.'

'My Dad was on the run once,' she confided. 'He—' She broke off, looking past him. 'Here comes Sarah.'

Mr Godfrey glanced round and saw the fair-haired girl approaching.

'Put your legs down, Elsie!' she said crossly, 'and stop showing everyone your knickers.'

Elsie's legs shot down so quickly that she lost her balance and fell off the stool. Sarah looked uncertainly at Mr Godfrey.

'He's all right . . . he's a friend,' said Elsie, picking herself up. 'I left me coat on the train and he brought it back.'

She lifted the coat from the stool where he'd laid it, swung it around her shoulders and with a wriggle and shake she was into it.

'That was very kind of you,' said Sarah politely. Her voice now was soft and there was a slight breathlessness to it that reminded him once again of Chick Courtney. It struck him that Elsie and Sarah were not at all alike for sisters.

'I'm starving!' Elsie declared. 'Can't we eat?'

'No, not yet. We must wait for Martin like we always do,' said Sarah.

Mr Godfrey was hungry himself but he didn't see that he could eat here—not with Elsie's eyes following every mouthful. He could depart now, leaving her safely in the care of her sister. First, though, he would clear up that piece of nonsense she'd trotted out.

'Elsie tells me she lives on the Tube,' he said to Sarah. He spoke light-heartedly in the way that he might have said 'Elsie says she believes in Father Christmas.'

Sarah gave her sister an angry look and Elsie squeaked:

'He won't tell no one 'cos he's on the run, aren't you, Arnold?'

He nodded tolerantly. 'She says you *all* live on the Underground. You . . . her . . . and your brother, Martin.' He smiled encouragingly, inviting her to dispel these wild imaginings of her young sister.

'Yes, that's right,' said Sarah calmly. 'We do.'

In the honeycomb of disused passages and tunnels behind Piccadilly Circus station, in a section not accessible to travellers, Butch, Sid and Terry grinned happily at one another. They had just dragged the bedrolls and haversacks from a new hiding place. It had taken them the whole afternoon to find them. They'd explored station after station and in the end they'd made their discovery almost literally beneath their feet at the station where they'd met each hour.

'I told you we'd find the stuff sooner or later,' Butch said.

'*I* found it,' Terry reminded him.

'Yeh, bully for you.' Butch gave him a friendly thump in the chest that sent the lightly-built Terry reeling. 'Now, let's take a butcher's.'

They unrolled the sleeping-bags and emptied the

contents of the haversacks onto the ground.

'Only clothes and a load of tat,' Sid grumbled when they'd finished pawing through everything.

'That old sod deserved the beating we give him then, didn't he?' said Terry fiercely. 'Bet he's aching a bit now, eh Butch?'

Butch Fearon glanced at him quickly. It was all right. Terry knew nothing. 'Yeh, I reckon so.' These two didn't read newspapers. Terry could hardly read at all. He pondered for a moment. 'There's a haversack missing,' he pointed out. 'The one with the packets of fags in it. We scared 'em last night and now they're carrying it around with them.'

'They'll have to come for their bedrolls tonight,' said Sid. 'Let's hang about.'

'Yeh, we'll take turns,' Butch agreed. 'But it's early yet. Let's grab a beer. My throat's as dry as an old tart's fanny.'

Carelessly they tramped through the possessions they had left strewn on the ground.

Mr Godfrey thought afterwards that he would probably never have become involved with the two girls if Sarah hadn't looked so much like a schoolgirl he'd once been fond of. When she became distressed it wrung his heart and he just had to help her.

Before he recovered from his astonishment at being told that the two girls not only roamed the Underground all day, but they actually *lived* on it, Sarah continued:

'I do wish Martin would hurry up.'

'S'pose he don't come?' Elsie asked.

'Don't be silly, of course he'll come.'

'P'raps the Skins got him again. P'raps he's *dead*.' Elsie's voice rose.

'Be *quiet*!' Sarah's face was white and her eyes filled

with tears. Mr Godfrey could hardly bear it when she said miserably, 'I don't know what to do.'

'You'd better tell me what the trouble is,' he said in a kindly tone. 'Look, I'm going to get a cup of tea and we'll all sit down. What would you two like?'

'Milk shake,' Elsie said promptly.

Sarah gave her a reproachful look. 'Thank you,' she said. 'A cup of tea for me and a milk shake for my sister.' She dragged her away to a vacant table.

'A *chocolate* one!' Elsie shouted from a distance.

When they were seated with the drinks Sarah began the story.

'Mum died a long time ago . . . when Elsie was born . . . and Dad looked after us. We were quite happy but then Dad was in trouble with the police and he ran away and left us. Martin said the Welfare people would put us in a Home—perhaps send us out to foster families and split us up. So we took off, Martin, Elsie and me, off into the country. That was last summer.'

'It was *lovely*,' Elsie said, letting go of her milk shake for a moment. 'We had a tent and sleeping-bags and—'

'Be quiet, Elsie! I'm telling the story,' Sarah said fiercely. 'Martin—he's almost grown up—he took jobs with holiday camps and places. We had a great time hitching from place to place. At the end of the summer, though, he couldn't find jobs and our money began to run out. And it was getting too cold for camping.' She picked up her cup and sipped the tea delicately.

Elsie seized her chance and butted in again. 'We flogged the tent and come back to London. I remember the day 'cos it was pouring of rain and Martin brought us on the trains to keep dry. He bought us crisps and comics and we went round and round the Circle while he thought what to do.'

Mr Godfrey nodded understandingly. He'd done the same thing himself yesterday.

Sarah put down her cup. 'Martin decided we'd have to spend the night on the Underground, so we started exploring the stations as we travelled about.'

Elsie said excitedly, 'D'you know . . . down there . . .' she pointed vaguely over her shoulder, ' . . . Oxford Circus . . . Piccadilly . . . stations like that, they have back stairs and tunnels no one knows about. There are *lots* of hiding places if you look for them.'

Sarah took up the tale again. They were performing a kind of duet, taking it in turns to continue the story. Sarah seemed to have given up over Elsie's interruptions. 'We chose a station with a comfy hideaway and when the trains stopped running and the station closed for the night we spread our bedrolls and went to sleep.'

'It was like they done in the War,' Elsie chimed in, rolling her eyes.

'How would *you* know?' Sarah demanded.

'I seen films about it on the telly!' Elsie's voice was shrill.

'Huh! Square-eyes!' Sarah snorted. 'You always watched the box too much. Anyway—' she went on '—as I was saying, we went to sleep. Next thing we knew we were woken up by the noise of the first train in the morning. It was half-past four!'

'We was *starving*,' Elsie put in.

'We left the Tube and found a workman's cafe and Martin spent nearly all our money on an enormous breakfast.'

'I still remember that brekkers,' said Elsie wistfully, nodding her head.

'What about tickets?' asked Mr Godfrey. 'You can't just wander on and off the Underground like that.'

'Martin bought returns to the next station from where we got on.'

'But tickets are date-stamped. You can't use the return half next day.'

They looked at him pityingly. 'Show him, Sarah,' Elsie suggested.

'Do you have a ticket on you?' Sarah asked.

'Yes, of course.' He handed her his ticket.

She licked her forefinger and rubbed hard at the date. 'There you are.'

He scrutinised the smudged figures. They were indecipherable.

'Ticket collectors never look at the date anyway,' Sarah said.

The girls continued their story. Martin had gone to look for casual work and Elsie and Sarah had spent the day on the Underground. All they had was a return ticket to the next station but they discovered they were able to wander all over the Underground system, changing lines, changing platforms, going anywhere they liked. Martin joined them later and once again they spent the night hidden in one of the stations.

Martin found a job and they continued to live in this fashion. The girls rode about during the day while Martin worked. They would stop off for food at one of the four snack bars on the Tube system and in the evening after work Martin would take them for a full meal. Later they would return to where they'd hidden their sleeping-bags and sleep on the Underground.

They soon understood the rail system thoroughly and knew most of its two hundred and fifty or so stations. They discovered many possible sleeping places including one or two at stations outside the central area which had heated waiting-rooms. At these outlying stations they would disappear into the lavatory just before the station closed for the night and emerge later to settle in a porter's cubbyhole or a warm waiting-room. At other times they would bed down in the labyrinth of back passages and emergency exits of a Tube station in Central London.

'It isn't so far for Martin to travel to work, then, you

see,' Sarah explained. 'And it's easier to find a place to hide our gear during the day. Otherwise we'd have to traipse it around with us.'

Martin was very strict about keeping clean and he regularly took their clothes to a laundrette. They became expert on where the best washing places and cleanest loos were to be found on the Underground system—not that there were very many available.

'You have to go miles for a pee sometimes,' Elsie complained. 'And that Baker Street loo—it's terrible of an evening. It *stinks!*'

Some days Martin set them tasks to do. Elsie would have to collect a copy of every daily newspaper—there were always plenty lying around after the rush-hour—and copy the headlines into her exercise book. Sarah might be told to write a summary of the day's news. On their journeys they methodically scavenged the carriages of every train they travelled on. Often there was money wedged in the crevices of the seats. The cigarette and sweet machines were another source of money as Elsie had already explained and it was a bad day when they didn't collect a handful of tenpence pieces from the reject coin slots. According to Elsie, who kept a tally in her little notebook, there were a hundred and three automatic machines on the Central Line alone. Sarah didn't believe that because, as she rudely put it, 'Elsie can't count for toffees.'

'But how long can you go on living like this?' Mr Godfrey asked.

'It's only until Martin has saved enough money. Then we're going to find a place to live,' Sarah said proudly. 'Maybe a caravan or a houseboat . . . something like that.'

'With proper beds,' added Elsie, 'and our own loo.'

'You'll need quite a bit of money for that,' Mr Godfrey warned.

'Martin will manage it,' Sarah said confidently. Her face

clouded. 'Only just when we were doing so well most of our savings have been stolen. It's not fair! Martin worked for weeks to save that money. He didn't carry it round with him in case of being mugged. We hid it in our gear.'

Mr Godfrey nodded sagely. 'What happened?'

'We ran into some Skinheads last night.' She shuddered. 'They'd searched our gear and found the money.' She described the encounter and the chase at Baker Street.

'I do wish Martin would come. He's never been as late as this before,' she said her face frowning in worry.

Four

Terry paused and cocked an ear as he was returning to the hiding-place. Butch had sent him down to keep first watch while he and Sid put away another pint. Again Terry heard something. He stepped quietly up the circular stairway that curled round an airshaft and led up to street level. On a landing halfway up, behind some bags which blocked the entrance to a side passage, was the place where they had made their find. He approached cautiously. The ginger-haired boy was kneeling down re-rolling the sleeping bags. The haversacks were neatly repacked and lying against the wall.

Terry bounded forward and then halted. The boy had risen to his feet and was watching him carefully. He was younger than Terry but he topped him by several inches and was broader in the chest. Terry was none too confident about tackling him on his own.

Scowling fiercely, he said. 'My mate's right behind. He wants to talk to you.'

'What about?'

'He'll tell you that hisself.'

The boy shrugged. 'Well, I don't want to talk to him.' He started to pick up the equipment.

'Put that down!' Terry ordered, advancing.

'It's ours,' the boy insisted.

Terry aimed a punch at his head. The boy ducked and chopped him sharply under the nose with the side of his hand. Wild with rage and pain, Terry flew at him, kicking and flailing and the boy retreated under the ferocity of the attack. Then, in a lucky moment, he side-stepped one of Terry's rushes and punched him on the side of the head. Terry's onward rush carried him forward into the wall where he crashed his head and fell to the floor.

Hastily the boy picked up the haversacks and, abandoning the bedrolls, ran away down the steps.

Shaking his head, Terry rose groggily to his feet. Butch would hammer him if the boy escaped. Groaning, he lurched off in pursuit.

'There's Martin now!' said Sarah, her face brightening. She waved through the window.

A youth with haversacks slung from his shoulder entered the cafe and sank into a vacant chair beside Mr Godfrey and the two girls. He had carrot-coloured hair and very pale blue eyes and Mr Godfrey put his age at fifteen or sixteen. His face bore a large red bruise on one cheek and his lip was split and puffy.

'What's happened to you?' Sarah asked anxiously.

'I had a bit of a fight, that's all.' He looked at Mr Godfrey. 'Who's this?'

'He's a friend,' said Elsie. 'His name's Arnold. He found me coat and we've been talking to him. He's on the run like Dad.'

'Daddy *isn't* on the run. They arrested him and put him in prison,' said Sarah.

'Well, he *was* on the run.'

Sarah let out a sigh of impatience and turned to her brother. 'Martin, where's the rest of our stuff?'

'I went to check that our gear was still OK. It had been pulled out and gone through again. While I was putting it straight one of those Skinheads came along. We had a punch-up and this was all I could bring away.'

'Where's me bedroll?' Elsie wailed. 'Where we gonna sleep?'

'Shut up Elsie while I think,' said Martin. 'We need a safe place. Where can we go?'

In a rush of sheer recklessness Mr Godfrey had the answer. With one instant decision he abandoned the life he knew. He turned his back on Mrs Godfrey, his home and unpleasant things like redundancy and shoplifting. He laughed wildly and three pairs of eyes stared at him.

'I know a place,' he said.

On the landing where Terry had fought with Martin, Butch stamped his boots angrily on the remnants of a blue sleeping-bag. A few moments before he had systematically slashed it into ribbons with his knife.

'He must've let 'em get away 'cos the haversacks is gone,' he snarled. 'Terry's gonna get my boot five lace-holes up his arse for this!'

'P'raps he's following 'em,' said Sid, 'and he'll find out where they've gone.'

'He better had,' Butch growled.

At Victoria Coach Station Mr Godfrey was buying tickets for them all. Martin heard him name the destination but it meant nothing to him. He was torn between fear of the Skinheads and what lay behind, and suspicion of Mr Godfrey and what lay ahead.

'Is it far to where you're taking us?' he asked as Mr Godfrey pocketed his change.

'Quite a way. It's in the country, you see.'

'Is it a house—*your* house?' Martin's voice was suddenly suspicious.

Mr Godfrey laughed, not at the question but at the thought of Mrs Godfrey's reaction if he turned up at home with this trio. She disliked children.

'No.' If he tried to explain, they wouldn't grasp what he meant—not until they'd been there and seen for themselves. Even then they wouldn't really understand, but that wouldn't matter. He hesitated, seeing the expression on the boy's face and appreciating the doubts going through his mind.

'Well, it's a *kind* of house,' he said, 'but it's under the ground and it's big—very big.' He had an inspiration. 'Like an air-raid shelter. Do you know what an air-raid shelter is?'

'*I* do,' Elsie piped. 'I seen films about air-raids on the telly. Everyone runs down them and hides away from the bombs. I love war films.'

'Is this an old air-raid shelter then?' Sarah asked.

'No. No it isn't. But I can't explain it better than that. Look—' he addressed them all '—you can always come back if you don't like the place.'

The two girls looked at Martin, awaiting his answer. *He* decided things like this, they didn't. Martin took Sarah aside.

'What d'you think, Sis? You've been chatting with him.'

'I think he's a nice old man and he's trying to help us.'

'But why should he? What's he want with us?'

'Well, he doesn't have anywhere to go himself and I expect he's lonely.'

'Elsie said he's in trouble. I wonder what he's done. It could be something dreadful.'

'Let's ask him.'

They rejoined Mr Godfrey. 'You told Elsie you're on the run from the police. What are they after you for?' asked Martin.

Mr Godfrey felt awkward under the scrutiny of the boy's frank blue eyes. If he told the exact truth they'd know the offence wasn't serious enough to send the police chasing after him; and he couldn't explain to them the complex reasons that had made him cut himself off from his present life. He didn't understand them himself. He compromised, choosing a word that sounded stronger than shoplifting.

'Thieving,' he said boldly, 'I've done some thieving.'

'That's like our Dad,' said Elsie cheerfully.

Martin gazed at Mr Godfrey's white hair and his open face with the spectacles slightly askew on his nose. He seemed nice enough and quite harmless. They had nowhere else to go. They'd have to trust him for the moment.

'OK,' he agreed. 'We've nothing to lose.'

As they boarded the Green Line bus standing in the bus station, a leather-jacketed figure slipped out through one of the exits into the street. Terry had been watching them, masked by the queues of people waiting for coaches. At Piccadilly Circus he'd staggered after Martin and managed to follow him to Liverpool Street without Martin seeing him. There he'd witnessed the link-up with Sarah and Elsie; but he'd been puzzled by the white-haired man sitting with the two girls. The old geezer looked spruce, not like a down-and-out. Terry knew that his only hope of redeeming himself with Butch Fearon and escaping a going-over would be to be able to tell him where he could find these three again; and therefore he'd followed them when they left the Liverpool Street cafe with Mr Godfrey.

Terry padded quickly along Eccleston Place. What he needed—urgent like—was wheels. Without wheels he couldn't follow the bus. Amid the parking meters he came to a section reserved for motor-cycles. He cast an expert eye over the machines and selected a Suzuki like his own, with a crash helmet dangling from the handlebars. He pushed it off its stand and wheeled it round the corner of the street. There he donned the crash helmet, started the bike and rode round the block to Ebury Street from where he could keep an eye on the vehicles leaving the Coach Station.

When the Reading bus pulled out with Mr Godfrey and the children on board Terry followed at a discreet distance on the stolen motor cycle.

Twilight was beginning when the Green Line bus stopped at Knowl Hill on the A4 beyond Maidenhead Thicket. Mr Godfrey and the three youngsters descended from the bus and crossed the road to the turning opposite which led to Warren Row. Very soon they were clear of the cluster of houses which comprised Knowl Hill. The road was deserted and the party walked in silence. Even Elsie stopped her chatter.

Mr Godfrey hurried them along because he was anxious to reach his objective before darkness fell. It had been nearly a year ago when he was last here and he wasn't sure of finding his way in the dark. There should be a wood soon. Then a wide, padlocked gate. Beyond the gate was a track leading into the wood and wide enough for vehicles.

They came to the gate and Mr Godfrey clambered over it followed by Martin. They waited for the girls.

Sarah hung back. The twilight was greying now. She had become increasingly uneasy as the last of the houses was left further and further behind. Mr Godfrey no longer seemed the kind old man they'd told their story to at Liverpool Street. As Elsie went to climb over the gate she pulled her back.

'This is as far as we go,' she said firmly, 'unless you tell us where you're taking us. Elsie and I aren't going into those woods to be raped.'

'What's *raped*?' Elsie squeaked.

Martin lowered his pack. 'It means he tears all your clothes off and sticks his thing into you.'

'*What* thing?' Elsie demanded.

'Never you mind,' said Sarah.

Mr Godfrey said impatiently, 'If we don't hurry I shan't be able to find the entrance in the dark. Look . . . you two girls stay here. Martin can come with me to see the place and then come back for you.'

Sarah nodded. 'Yes, all right.'

As he set off with Martin Elsie's breathy whispers floated after him. 'But Sarah, he could still *strangle* Martin . . . and then he could creep back . . . and then. . . .' The rest of her dreadful imaginings were lost on the evening air.

Behind them, on the A4, came the distant roar of a motorcycle speeding along through Knowl Hill and past the stop where they had left the bus. The sound of its engine died away towards Reading. Terry was racing to catch up with the Green Line bus. At Maidenhead Thicket, just after the roundabout, his engine had spluttered and died. It had taken only a moment or two to locate the trouble. It was diabolical, Terry grumbled, the way people neglected their bikes and let the carburettor get full of muck. He'd been away again within a few minutes but in that time the bus had drawn two or three miles ahead. Terry hadn't expected to have to travel this far when he'd set out to follow Martin but having come all this way he wasn't giving up now.

Deep in the wood at Warren Row Mr Godfrey came to the high chain-link fencing of the perimeter. The track continued alongside the fence to some heavy, padlocked iron gates that were as tall as the fence. Martin peered curiously through the bars. There was nothing to be seen beyond the gates except trees and undergrowth. The track turned in through the gates and then sloped downwards into the ground to the left and out of view.

'Come along,' Mr Godfrey urged, moving on, 'we can't get in that way.'

'What's in there?' Martin asked.

'You'll see,' was all Mr Godfrey answered.

They continued along the fence. The going was more difficult now that the track had ended and the undergrowth grew right up to and even through the fence. They came to a corner where the fence turned at right angles away from them. Mr Godfrey paused, staring into the gloom under the trees. It was almost dark and he chewed his lips in anxiety. Everywhere had looked different in daylight. He plunged into the bushes, trying hard to maintain a straight course as he skirted trees and blackberry bushes.

After about fifty yards he halted and looked about him. Suppose he couldn't find what he was looking for? All at once he felt very responsible for the three young people who were depending on him. Standing there, uncertain how to proceed, he realised how crazy the whole idea was. Martin was carefully keeping his distance, obviously not trusting him. In desperation, Mr Godfrey began tramping round in a circle. It had to be here somewhere. Then, with an exclamation of relief, he saw his objective.

Martin joined him and gazed sceptically at the square-shaped concrete block protruding about a foot above the ground. There was a metal trap door across the top and thick wire mesh covered apertures at the sides.

'That's just a drain,' he observed in disgust.

'It's an airshaft,' Mr Godfrey corrected. 'The only one outside the perimeter fence.' He cast around, picked up a stout stick and levered it under the lid of the trap.

'That's solid steel,' Martin commented.

'Yes, but I happen to know there's only one small bolt inside holding it shut.'

He leaned his weight on the stick and with a metallic bang the bolt fixing snapped off. He lifted the trapdoor and laid it back on its hinges. Martin stared down into the gaping darkness. The poor light revealed iron rungs leading down. He shivered, suddenly reminded of a murder case he'd read about. A young heiress had been kidnapped and kept prisoner in a shaft like that. Her naked body had been found hanging by the neck from a wire attached to one of the rungs. He stepped away as Mr Godfrey lowered himself inside and disappeared from sight. After a moment or two a shaft of light shot upwards, cutting the darkness. Martin moved to the rim and looked down. At the bottom of the shaft which was some twenty feet deep a light had been switched on. There was a doorway to one side which Mr Godfrey was now opening. He signalled Martin to come down. The boy hesitated. Then, laying his haversack on the ground, he descended.

A mile or two away Terry caught up with the bus near Kiln Green. The interior lights were on now and he saw that the downstairs seats where his quarry had sat were vacant. They must have left the bus at the last stop. He slowed the bike and did a U turn. Gunning the engine he headed back towards Knowl Hill.

Martin watched Mr Godfrey lift a battery lantern from a hook on the wall inside the door and step into a short passage that seemed, in the glow of the lantern, to have been hewn out of solid chalk. There was a steel door at the end of the passage with hand levers at top and bottom. Martin followed Mr Godfrey and stood behind him as he pushed down the two handles and pulled open the door. Six feet along the passage was another, identical, door.

'Airlocks,' Mr Godfrey explained, opening the second door and stepping through. In the light of the lantern reflected from the chalk Martin became aware of a cavernous area with a tunnel-shaped roof and piping and ducts running everywhere. Underfoot the chalk floor had been asphalted.

'This is the air-conditioning plant,' Mr Godfrey said, his voice echoing in the silence. 'It's not on, of course.' He

continued through the Plant-Room, swinging the beam of
light ahead of him.

They came to a brick wall across the tunnel with a door
in it. On a shelf beside the door were two more lanterns.
Mr Godfrey picked one up, switched it on and handed it
to Martin. He opened the door and they walked through.
The tunnel continued beyond the wall and it had been
divided into rooms by hardboard partitioning on either
side of a central corridor. The partitions were six feet high
and reached less than halfway to the chalk roof of the
tunnel. The doorways to the rooms had no doors in them
and the windows onto the corridor were simply rectangu-
lar panels cut out of the hardboard.

Mr Godfrey shone the light into one of the rooms and
Martin saw bunks, mattresses and folded blankets. They
moved to the next section which was fitted out as a
kitchen with a cooker and a sink.

'You'll be very comfortable here—and safe,' said Mr
Godfrey. He pointed the torch beam down the corridor.
'And there's a food store along there.'

'What *is* this place?' Martin asked wonderingly.

'I'll explain later. Now, you go back and collect the
girls—they'll be frightened out there in the dark—and I'll
get the lights on.'

'OK.' Martin turned and retraced his steps to the
airshaft.

Up above, Terry had arrived at the Knowl Hill stop. He
rode several hundred yards further on and then returned
to the stop. He sat astride his machine, feet planted on the
ground, gazing thoughtfully at the turning opposite. Of
course the old man and the kids could already have
entered one of the houses around here but, if not. . . . He
revved the engine, shot across the A4 and careered along
the road to Warren Row.

Sarah and Elsie climbed over the gate and followed
Martin as he led the way into the wood. Suddenly there

was the staccato bark of an approaching motorcycle engine and they instinctively turned their heads towards the gate behind them. A headlight sliced the darkness, its reflected glare reaching out into the wood, lighting their pale faces for an instant as the motor cycle flashed past. Terry had missed them by seconds.

Down below, Mr Godfrey had proceeded along the tunnel to where it was joined by another, smaller tunnel. He entered the room where the master switches were housed and played his torch on the panel of knobs and circuit switches, studying it . . . remembering. He flicked down a large, lever-type switch and there was a blaze of overhead light.

Smiling, he stepped through into the Operations Room.

Five

Two years ago. That was the first time he'd set foot in this place. It had all seemed so important then. He remembered the secrecy and the sense of urgency. That, and the feeling of underlying dread—a kind of awful thrill at the thought that *this* might really be *it*; that this international crisis might just be the one that would lead to the Third World War and to a nuclear holocaust.

There had been crises before, of course: the Berlin Wall; the Cuban Missile crisis. Indeed it was the occurrence of those events which had first led to the hurried conversion of this one-time chalk quarry into an underground operational headquarters. The grandiose title—REGIONAL SEAT OF GOVERNMENT—belied its rough and ready accommodation and the simple equipment. If the unthinkable happened this would be the place from which London—or what was left of it after a nuclear attack—would be controlled. Here would sit the Regional Commissioner, his military advisers, the police and civil defence chiefs and the top men of all the civil organisations. They would be trying to co-ordinate their efforts to deal with survivors and the smouldering ruins of the stricken capital. Similar Regional Seats of Government in other parts of the country would be doing the same for their areas.

Two essentials were: the headquarters had always to be ready for immediate use; and staff trained to use it had to be instantly available. To meet the first requirement it was fitted out with equipment and sufficient supplies to enable it to function entirely cut off, except for communications, from the rest of the country for three months, if necessary.

Much thought had gone into providing what was necessary for the fifty or so staff of men and women who would man the bunker to subsist underground for that length of time. Apart from protection against radioactive fallout, filtering the air supply and things like that, attention had also been given to other little essentials for improving the quality of life underground.

'D'you know,' commented a girl wireless operator, ogling a husky engineer she rather fancied, 'there's even a cabinet of contraceptives—all different kinds!'

The staff to operate the headquarters were selected from volunteers among staff of the various Town Halls in London. Arnold Godfrey had gladly volunteered and was pleased when he was accepted for training as an operations clerk. His particular task in the Operations Room was to plot information on the maps there. Since that time, two years ago, he'd spent many a happy week-end away from Mrs Godfrey, deep underground at Warren Row taking part in training exercises. He wasn't sure that she believed his story—especially as he wasn't allowed to tell her very much about what he was doing. She called it 'playing at War' which made his efforts sound trivial and childish.

He hadn't learned about the 'escape' hatch until the last training exercise a year ago. On that occasion the Controller-Designate—the man who would run the Operations Room in War—had asked them, as an experiment, to do without the air-conditioning for twenty-hours. He wanted to test what conditions would be like if the plant failed, or if the filters became clogged with radioactive fallout dust from distant nuclear explosions and had to be closed down. After a while the effect of so many people being closeted underground without a supply of fresh air had proved to be pretty unpleasant. Arnold Godfrey had finished his shift in the Operations Room and was off duty resting in his bunk when one of the other plotting clerks spoke to him.

'How would you like to go outside for some clean air, a draught beer and a break from this monotony?'

'Wouldn't I just,' Mr Godfrey sighed. 'But we can't. The entrance is sealed off.'

'There's another way out.'

'There can't be. I don't believe it.'

'Come on. I'll show you.' He led Mr Godfrey to the Plant-Room and out through the two airlocks to the rough passage in the chalk beyond. At the end of the passage they'd come to the bottom of the shaft. So real had been the exercise down below, that they almost believed they were emerging into a dust-ridden radioactive countryside as they slipped through the woods in the dark to the local pub.

The other clerk had been with the team from the beginning, before the work on improvising the head-quarters had been finished. He told Arnold Godfrey how the escape shaft came into existence. After the work on the chalk quarry had ended it was realised that if there were a fire during an exercise, staff were bound to be trapped in the section of tunnel on the other side of the fire from the entrance. So, as a temporary solution, a shaft had been sunk to meet the bottom end of the tunnel and provide an emergency exit. By that time the perimeter fence above ground had already been erected and it couldn't be helped that the escape shaft was outside the security fence. It had been intended to construct a proper fire exit from another part of the tunnel but the international emergency had passed and work on the bunker ceased. Later the exercises had stopped, Civil Defence had been disbanded and the government department concerned merely kept the bunker in a state of readiness for the next emergency.

Mr Godfrey was recalled to the present by the rattle of feet on the iron rungs as Elsie, twittering and complaining, struggled down the shaft. Martin escorted the two girls, wide-eyed, through the Plant-Room and into the living area, everywhere now brilliantly lit by strip-lights. They wandered around, poking and prying.

'This is a bit like the Underground,' Martin commented, staring up at the curved roof which he could now see clearly with the lights on.

'It's much better than the Tube, though, it has *everything*,' said Sarah in wonderment.

'I bet it hasn't got a telly,' Elsie grumbled.

'Actually, there are two,' Mr Godfrey told her, feeling an unexpected pride in the place. 'One in the Recreation Room and one in the canteen.

Elsie's face lit up. 'Show me.' She tugged at his arm.

'Later, Elsie,' said Martin. 'Now will you tell us what this place is?' he asked.

They gazed expectantly at Mr Godfrey. He hesitated, thinking he shouldn't tell them too much. A coy loyalty and an old-fashioned attitude to security, restrained him. After all, he *had* signed one of those buff forms binding himself to secrecy under the Official Secrets Act. Cautiously, he explained in a very general way. They sat on the bunks and listened. Half-way through, Elsie, bored with all the talk, started to yawn.

'I'm tired,' she moaned. 'I wanna go to bed.' Moments later her head drooped and she began snoring. Sarah gently pushed her down and laid a blanket over her.

'I don't understand how it keeps warm and dry down here,' Martin said.

49

'There are storage heaters connected to temperature and humidity controls. And the engineer calls in regularly to air the place.'

'What's the gun for?' Sarah asked abruptly.

'Gun?' queried Mr Godfrey, startled.

'Yes. There's a gun clipped on a board on the wall at the bottom of the steps where we came in.'

'Oh, *that.*' He laughed. 'That's not really a gun. It's a Very pistol—a flare pistol. The idea was that if we had to evacuate the place quickly because of a fire, we'd discharge a flare into the air to attract attention.'

'I see.' She looked at her watch. 'It's very late. I'll make some cocoa.' She went to the cupboard. 'Tinned or powdered milk?' She might have been a hostess asking if you wanted brown or white sugar in your coffee.

'Tinned, please,' said Mr Godfrey.

'Powdered,' said Martin.

They exchanged smiles. We're playing mothers and fathers, thought Mr Godfrey.

The clink of cups woke Elsie. 'I wanna do pee-pees,' she announced.

Sarah took her along the corridor to the lavatories.

'Where does all the pee-pees go?' Elsie wanted to know when she returned.

'To a sump. A big tank,' Mr Godfrey explained. 'Eventually, it's pumped out into a tanker and taken away.'

Soon after, they went to bed. The two girls shared a cabin and Mr Godfrey and Martin had separate ones. Mr Godfrey was unable to sleep for some time. He felt a strange elation. This hadn't been a crazy idea after all. It was going to work. It was like being a family. He liked that. He'd always wanted a family.

They were waiting for Terry when he arrived back at his mum's later that night.

'Your mum's round the pub with her latest bedmate, old son,' Butch told him, emerging from the shadows as Terry opened the door to the ground-floor flat where he lived.

'We just come from there,' added Sid, putting an arm across the door in front of Terry and preventing him from entering. 'She said you hadn't bin home all evening.'

'Yeh, where you bin since you left us at the 'Dilly? That was terrible rude, Terry. Shockin' manners. That weren't polite.' Butch gave him a playful push that sent him reeling into the wall. 'Let 'em get away, did you?'

'No, listen Butch, I—'

'Know where they are then, do you?' Butch seized Terry's collar and twisted it up under his chin, half-choking him. Terry saw the shine in the eyes only inches away from his own. Any second Butch would jerk his leg violently upwards and knee him in the balls.

'Yeh! Yeh! I do know where they are!' he babbled. He poured out his story, giving his own version of the encounter with Martin. 'He jumped me, Butch, that's how he got away. But I followed him.' Quickly he related the evening's events.

When he'd finished Butch kicked the wall thoughtfully with the toe of his boot. 'So you reckon they're in a house close to that bus stop, eh?'

'They must be. Stands to reason,' said Terry, breathing more easily now that he wasn't going to get a drubbing. 'They can't be more'n a few minutes walk away. Maybe that old geezer they met was their grandaddy and they live there.'

Butch thought for a bit longer. 'Right, then!' He stamped his foot decisively on the concrete path and sparks flew from the metal studs on the soles. 'Tomorrow's Saturday. You nick some wheels Terry, and pick me and Sid up first thing.'

'Is it worth the bother, Butch?' Sid asked.

51

'Yeh. I still think they've got a lot of loot with 'em.' He spat. 'We'll have a nice day in the country. It'll be a gig. An' like I told you, I want that blonde hole.'

'She's only a kid, Butch.'

'She's old enough!' he snarled.

Six

Mr Godfrey woke early after a bad night. He'd kept asking himself what he was trying to do; and he'd spent some time reflecting on his life and what he'd achieved, or rather not achieved. He wasn't used to self-analysis and he found it a painful business.

What was there to look forward to? Death, of course. Death was always there waiting, drawing nearer as you grew older. Death came mostly by accident to the young and the middle-aged and the chances of it were quite small. When you were old though, death stalked you closer each month that passed. And the quicker the months slipped by, the quicker death hurried to meet you.

What would he leave behind? *Nothing.* Nothing to mark the sixty, seventy, or however many years he might live. Nothing to mark his coming and going. Nothing left but sprinkled ashes in the Garden of Remembrance at some crematorium. He hadn't written a play or a novel. He hadn't built anything. There had been no great romance in his life, no wonderful experience. He left no children, no heirs. Perhaps if he and Mrs Godfrey had had children his life wouldn't have seemed so meaningless. Something of himelf would have been left behind to be passed on. As it was, the only dramatic events in his personal life had occurred in the last few weeks. He'd been made redundant and, yesterday, he'd been charged with theft.

As he dressed he cast a rueful eye over his suit. Office suits weren't designed for sleeping in on railway stations or in underground bunkers. He'd better help himself to a civil defence battledress from the clothing store as well as some clean underclothes.

He looked in on the two girls and marvelled at how they could sleep so soundly in strange surroundings. But then if you were used to sleeping in odd corners on the London Underground, he supposed you could sleep anywhere. He'd found the bunks rather uncomfortable himself, but Elsie and Sarah would think them blissful of course. Elsie lay with her head lolling over the side of her bunk, half falling out. He tried to ease her into a safer position and she opened her eyes and sighed.

'What's for brekkers?' she mumbled. She turned over and went to sleep again without waiting for an answer.

He strolled along the tunnel towards the real entrance. It was all of a hundred yards, up a gentle slope. There were large double doors of steel across the entrance, wide enough to admit a vehicle and fastened on the outside with massive padlocks. He entered the small office beside the entrance and examined the engineer's logbook. This was a foolscap diary in which the engineers made an entry each time they visited the site. There seemed to be two separate cycles of visits: one by the wireless engineer who serviced the communications equipment and the other by the maintenance engineer who looked after the power supplies and the generating equipment. From the entries it didn't seem as though the site was due for another visit from either of them for a while. That was one worry less, thought Mr Godfrey.

He returned to the living area and found Sarah fully at home in the kitchen.

'I can manage, thank you,' she told him when he

offered to help. 'I did all the cooking when we were camping. It's only a matter of getting used to an electric cooker—I've never cooked on electric before.'

After breakfast Martin asked: 'How long can we stay here?'

'As long as we like as far as I can see.'

'Oh, goody!' cried Elsie, who was happy now that she'd located the television sets.

'Won't the food run out?' Sarah asked.

'There's enough of everything to last fifty people for three months.'

'Yes, but how long will it last *us*?' Sarah persisted.

'Perhaps Martin will do the arithmetic for us,' suggested Mr Godfrey in a schoolmasterish tone. 'If food lasts fifty people three months how long will it last four people?'

Martin looked uncomfortable. 'I don't know. A long time I guess.'

Mr Godfrey puffed out his cheeks. He hadn't meant to embarrass the boy and he was shocked to discover that he couldn't do a simple sum like that.

'Well, it's fifty times three divided by four. That's thirty-seven and a half months. Over three years.'

'Three *years*?' they echoed.

'At least.'

Sarah looked thoughtful. She had been applying a housewifely mind to the situation. 'Are you sure we have everything we need? What about bread?'

'There are ingredients for making your own—and instructions on how to do it,' he told her cheerfully. He knew the contents of the foodstore very well. On the last exercise he'd done a stint in the canteen. 'There are no fresh vegetables, of course, only tinned. But there's nothing to prevent us buying a few things at the local shops if we wish. I have some money.'

'What about sweeties?' Elsie asked. 'I bet there's no sweeties.'

'Yes, there's barley sugar, chewing-gum and chocolate.'

'Ice cream?' she challenged.

'No, no ice cream I'm afraid,' Mr Godfrey replied patiently.

'Ice cream's my favourite pud,' she moaned.

'Oh, shut up, Elsie,' said Martin. 'This is an absolutely marvellous place for us.'

Terry didn't understand at first why Butch had brought a slag like Big Marion along with him on Saturday morning. Marion would do anything you asked but she was an ugly tart and as thick as two planks and he knew Butch didn't fancy her one little bit.

When they arrived at Knowl Hill and Butch began briefing her in the car, his purpose became clear.

'We gotta use a bit of brain,' he growled. 'Ain't no use Sid and Terry and me wandering around looking for them kids. We'd scare everyone off. *You're* gonna do the visiting, doll.' He put an arm round Marion's waist, reached up and squeezed her ample breast. She gave a grunt of pleasure.

'You knock on every door,' he went on, 'and you say "Excuse me" . . . very polite, see? "Excuse me", you say, "but I'm looking for three friends of mine who came here yesterday. A ginger boy, a tall, blonde girl and a little dark-haired one. Do you know where they are, please?" Got that, doll?'

Marion nodded slowly. 'Yes, Butch, I got it.' She gazed at him with limpid eyes.

'Then say it all back to me.'

He made her repeat the words several times until she was word-perfect; and she had to practise a nice smile to go with the words until he was satisfied with the total result. Then Butch pushed her out of the car and, with a hard slap on her backside, sent her ambling off like a cow out of a milking-stall.

By midday Butch was exasperated. Marion had flopped

into the rear seat with her latest report. She had covered nearly every house in the village and no one had heard of, or seen, the trio.

'You *sure* this was where they got off, Terry?' Butch demanded.

'It *has* to be. They was on the bus the stop *before* here and they wasn't on it when I caught it up at the one *after*.'

Butch sat glowering, not enjoying his day in the country. Beside him, Marion oozed perspiration.

'I've been beating me gums all morning,' she croaked, 'and I'm parched.'

'So'm I!' Butch said peevishly. 'Where's the nearest pub?'

'There's one about a mile up the road over there,' Terry told him. 'At a place called Warren Row. I passed it last night.'

Two hours later, at closing time, the Skinheads and Marion fell out of the bar of the pub laughing and belching and very full of drink. After an argument over who was driving, Terry took the wheel. Sid sat beside him and Marion and Butch collapsed into the rear seats.

As they drove back towards Knowl Hill Marion plastered Butch's thick lips with slobbery, open-mouthed kisses. She thrust her hands down inside his belt to fondle him and Butch, in his alcoholic haze, began to think she was worth his attention after all.

They passed a padlocked gate on the wooded road and he caught a flash of bright colour in the woods, a splash of blue against the reds and browns of autumn. He pushed Marion away roughly and sat up, focusing his eyes.

'Slow down, me old mate,' he ordered Terry. 'I think we just struck lucky.'

They followed his pointing finger. Elsie's light-blue dress stood out sharply. Beside her was Sarah in navy blue jumper and skirt, her long hair shining like gold.

'It's them,' breathed Butch. 'Drive on and pull off the

road out of sight. I don't want no slip-ups this time. We'll creep up on them. Marion, you stay with the motor.'

'I'm cold, I'm going in,' said Elsie.

'You should have put on your coat if you were cold,' Sarah said sternly.

'I wasn't cold down there, was I?' Elsie retorted.

'Oh, all right, go on,' Sarah said impatiently. 'I'll be down in a minute. I want to pick some evergreen to brighten things up. I'm going to look for holly.'

Elsie trotted off and by the time the Skinheads returned to the wood she had vanished down the open shaft.

'That's the blonde girl all right, but the little one's disappeared,' Terry observed as they crouched in the undergrowth watching Sarah.

'That's a pity,' Butch grinned. 'I was gonna give her to you, Terry.'

'She's about his size,' Sid gurgled, 'but d'you think he'd know what to do with her?'

'Shut your gob!' Terry said fiercely.

'Belt up, both of you,' Butch commanded. 'Keep your minds on catching this blonde bit. You, Sid—you creepy-crawl round behind her. Terry—you go to the right. I'll come at her from the front. And don't neither of you pissy bastards stand up till I do!'

Sarah had found a holly bush and was stretching out a hand to it when the close-cropped head of Butch Fearon rose up out of the undergrowth in front of her. She recognised him instantly and froze.

'Hully, kiddo.' He gave her a lop-sided grin.

She glanced quickly around. Sid came to his feet behind her. To her left, between her and the escape shaft, stood Terry.

'Where's your ginger boyfriend, then?' asked Butch.

'He's not a boyfriend, he's my brother!' she snapped. 'What are you doing here? Why don't you leave us alone?'

'OK, doll, so he's your brother. Where is he?'

'What do you want?'

'Teach you both a lesson.' He belched loudly and the other two guffawed. Butch had already lost interest in Martin or the money for the moment. Inflamed with alcohol all his attention was centred on the long-legged girl standing defiantly in front of him.

'You first,' he added thickly. He pulled a long knife from the sheath on his belt and pointed it at her. Sarah drew in her breath.

'Get 'em down!' he ordered.

She pretended not to understand. 'I—I—don't know what you mean.'

'You know all right. Get your pants off, doll. You'll talk better without 'em.' He roared with drunken laughter and the other two brayed like donkeys.

Sarah knew it would be useless screaming. There was no one who would help her near enough to hear. If she ran they'd be on her like a pack of dogs. Her escape route to the shaft away to her left was blocked by the smallest of the Skinheads. But they didn't know the shaft existed and it was her only hope.

'Hurry up!' Butch hiccupped. 'Take 'em right off and get your skirt up.'

Terry whinnied with excitement. Butch's hard-on showed plainly through his jeans. He wouldn't be content with finger-fucking this one. He'd go all the way like the time he rodded that Punk bitch behind the cinema. He moved round for a better view, ready to grab her when Butch gave the signal.

As he changed his position Sarah saw her escape path opening up. Shaking with fear she assessed direction and distance. There would be no second chance. Their eyes were riveted on her as she bent and reached under her skirt.

She straightened, flung herself sideways and ran like

the wind, gaining precious seconds from their surprise. They recovered and she heard them whooping and baying as they pounded after her. Sobbing for breath she reached the top of the shaft and clambered down in frantic haste. There was no time to pull the trap shut and fiddle with the peg of metal Mr Godfrey had provided to secure it in place of the broken bolt. But she only had to go through the door at the bottom and along the short passage and she'd be able to shout for Martin and Mr Godfrey.

Sarah jumped off the bottom rung and fell against the door. It didn't move. In a panic she twisted the handle and threw her weight against it. Still it wouldn't budge. *The door was jammed.* Perhaps Elsie had slammed it carelessly when she went through and it had accidentally wedged itself. Sarah hammered on the door with her hands although she knew they wouldn't be able to hear her in the bunker. She began to cry.

Seven

The daylight at the top of the shaft was suddenly blotted out. Sarah looked up. Three cropped heads peered down at her.

'What's down there?' Sid asked Butch.

'Dunno. Looks like a drain. C'mon up, Blondie,' he called, 'You're trapped.'

Sarah flattened herself against the wall in terror.

'P'raps it's an old well,' Terry suggested.

'No, it—' Butch broke off and yelped with laughter. 'Yeh, a *well*! Well, well, well. . . .' The others took up the chant. 'Pussy in the well.' They fell about howling with glee at the joke.

'Th-there's a p-pussy in the well!' Butch slapped his leg and doubled up with mirth. 'Tell you what.' He struggled to unfasten his trousers. 'Let's get rid of some of that beer.' He snorted helplessly. 'Come on, mates! Piss up and fill the well!'

Sarah screamed as the foul-smelling stream poured down on her. She dodged to one side but a second stream splashed down, catching her in the face and soaking her hair, as Sid joined in.

'Mine's going up,' Terry giggled. 'I'm still stiff.'

'Bend forward you silly bugger!' Butch chortled as he lurched about directing his flow.

Sarah waved her hands hysterically above her head trying to shield herself. The deluge ended and Butch's voice bellowed:

'Jus' givin' it a shake, darlin', then I'm coming down to give your pussy a treat.'

Demented, she hurled herself at the door again. It was as immovable as before. She saw the flare pistol clipped to a board on the wall beside her and yanked it free, staring wild-eyed at its massive 1" bore, ready-loaded with a cartridge. All Sarah knew about guns was that you pointed them and pulled the trigger.

With shaking hands she aimed upwards to where Butch Fearon stood with legs astride the opening, about to descend on her. She squeezed the trigger but the action was heavy and the hammer hardly lifted. Grasping the butt with both hands she hooked her two forefingers round the trigger and pulled again.

With an ear-splitting roar in the confined space, the Very cartridge hurtled from the barrel. Designed to soar 150 feet into the air before bursting, and then to cascade to earth, it travelled only twenty feet before it smashed into Butch Fearon's crutch. The force of the impact hurled him backwards and the flare lodged in his open flies, disintegrating, spilling out and burning with intense heat and a brilliant, greenish-white light.

Butch began screaming. He went on screaming for three whole minutes before he became unconscious. His companions watched, appalled, as he writhed on the ground, shrieking and jerking, his crotch blazing like a Roman Candle. They tried to remove his jeans but had to retreat with burned hands. They took off their jackets and beat at the flames but the flare would not be extinguished until it had burned for its allotted time.

When it was over and he at last lay still they faced each other with gaunt eyes. Sickened by the stench of burnt flesh they knelt beside the unconscious body.

'We gotta get him to hospital quick,' Sid moaned.

'Yeh.' Terry pulled at the charred material on Butch's thigh and it came away with flesh sticking to it. *'Christ!'* He turned his head and vomited on the ground.

Lifting Butch by arms and feet they bore him to the car as fast as they could and laid him on the rear seat. Marion took one look before they covered him with a blanket, and went into hysterics.

'What's happened? What's happened?' she gabbled. 'He smells like—oh, gawd—' She gulped. Then her eyes rolled up into her head and she began to laugh insanely.

'Belt up, you silly cow!' Sid hit her full in the mouth. She stopped the noise at once, a comical, puzzled expression on her face.

'Move over! We'll all sit in the front. Terry, you drive.'

'Yeh, but where to Sid?'

'Look for a 'phone. We'll put in a 999 call for an ambulance and leave him there covered with a blanket. Then we'll beat it back to London and dump the car.'

It was Martin who discovered Sarah, curled up in a state of shock, lying in the stinking wet at the bottom of the escape shaft. Elsie had returned to look for her after a while when she hadn't followed her down. Unable to open the door to the shaft, she'd fetched Martin. He'd freed the door and found Sarah.

After her first, halting explanation Mr Godfrey stopped Martin questioning her further because Sarah was becoming more and more upset.

'Can't you see the state your sister's in, Martin? Let her clean up and calm down. We can talk about this later.' Sarah gave him a grateful look.

An hour or so on, when she had recovered, they discussed the attack.

'How badly was he hurt?' Mr Godfrey asked when she

described shooting the flare pistol at the leader of the Skinheads.

'I don't know,' she answered wretchedly. 'He made a terrible noise . . . for a long time.' She had cowered in the shaft, covering her ears to shut out that dreadful shrieking.

'P'raps you killed him,' Elsie suggested with her usual child's directness.

'No!' Sarah looked aghast and turned to Mr Godfrey. 'You can't kill someone with a flare, can you?' she asked agitatedly.

'I don't know—but I'm sure you didn't,' he told her reassuringly. No point in dwelling on the possible fatal injuries that could be inflicted by a burning flare. The girl was disturbed enough already.

'Do you think they'll return, Sis?' Martin asked.

'No, not after—' She paused and then continued: 'They thought the shaft was a drain or a well. They've no idea it leads anywhere and I think it was just bad luck they saw me in the woods. They can't know we're down here.'

'I wonder how they came to be here at all, though,' Martin said, frowning.

'It does seem an extraordinary coincidence,' Mr Godfrey observed. 'Perhaps the one you had a fight with followed us.'

'Yes, but why? What do they want?'

'Goodness knows. But whatever the reason we must be especially careful for a while. If anyone wants to go up top we'll all go together.'

A week went by and then another without any sign of the Skinheads. They relaxed and settled into a daily routine. After breakfast there were lessons and, in the afternoon, a walk across the Downs. Then more lessons until supper. In the evening they played games and watched television.

The lessons were Martin's idea. Mr Godfrey thought it was touching how Martin worried about the schooling the girls were missing—considering how little education the lad himself seemed to have had. He couldn't even do simple arithmetic. The lessons began as a continuation of the exercises Martin had set for the girls when they were riding about on the Tube all day. However, they developed into a kind of voluntary education programme. Freed of their worries and fears, and with time on their hands, the children seemed to want to study things that interested them.

Sarah started to collect wildflowers and different grasses and Martin became absorbed in electronics. Mr Godfrey knew very little about these subjects but he did his best to encourage and he bought one or two books for them.

The walks across the countryside often turned into long rambles and were an essential part of their routine. Not only did they get very little exercise in their underground home, but they were entirely shut off from the daylight and it was vital to their well-being to take regular walks above ground. There was a minor complication about the time. All the clocks in the bunker were twenty-four hour clocks and they had to accustom themselves to these, otherwise they wouldn't have known whether it was night or day up above.

The games they played in the evening were a revelation to the children. There was a wide selection in the cupboard in the Recreation Room: Monopoly, Scrabble, Mastermind, Chess and many other games.

'Haven't you played *any* of these before?' Mr Godfrey asked them in exasperation as they argued over what to play and started through the rules of Monopoly. Sarah shook her head.

Martin said, 'I tried chess at school once, but didn't understand it.'

'I don't like games, I'd sooner watch telly,' Elsie proclaimed.

'That's because you don't know how to play,' said Sarah.

'Let's try Scrabble,' Mr Godfrey suggested. 'We can all join in that.'

Those first weeks were like a breath of fresh air in Mr Godfrey's life. He'd always wanted a place in the country and he'd always longed for a family. Now he had both. He was very happy. The children too seemed happy with this new life. He told himself that the routine was good for them and no doubt brought stability to their disordered lives.

'I don't suppose he'll be able to get it up so easy then for a bit,' said Terry, staring glumly into his glass of beer as he raised it to his mouth. He and Sid had been to see Butch in the hospital in Reading. It had been a depressing visit and they were trying to cheer themselves up with a few pints before returning to London.

'You ain't grasped what I'm telling you,' said Sid. 'He won't be getting it up *at all* . . . not *ever*. While you was having your gab with Butch I chatted up that little spade nurse . . . the one who wobbled her arse all the time. She told me his nuts was burned right off.'

Terry put down his glass unsteadily. 'You mean—' His eyes went wide in horror. 'You mean he's got no bollocks?'

'That's it.' Sid nodded. 'They've docked his pecker too. It was all shrivelled and they had to amputate it. They left him a stump to piddle through, though.'

Terry shuddered. *'Jesus!'* He took a long draught of his beer. 'Did he tell them how it happened?'

'He said it was an accident and he'd been fooling around with a home-made firework.'

'What do you reckon it was really, Sid? I mean, what did she have down that sewer?'

'It *must* have been a firework of some sort—a rocket, maybe. It wasn't long after Guy Fawkes night. Butch was plumb unlucky it got him in the cobblers.'

Terry wiped his mouth with the back of his hand. 'He's taking it pretty well, considering.'

'He don't know,' said Sid bleakly. 'They ain't told him yet. He's all bandaged up down there and so's his hands, so he don't know what's what.'

'Jesus, it'll blow his mind when they tell him!'

Sid nodded. 'He'll go right round the twist.'

Mournfully shaking their heads, they gulped noisily at their drinks.

'I do love it here,' Elsie said contentedly. She was sitting in front of the television spooning ice-cream into her mouth. Sarah had discovered a way of making ice-cream in the freezer compartment of the fridge using a mixture of custard powder and tinned milk. No one else thought the result was much like the real thing but it satisfied Elsie.

Mr Godfrey looked up from his book and smiled. They'd taken to using one of the Recreation Rooms as a living-room and sitting in it together of an evening. Sarah was doing the ironing and Martin was reading.

Elsie's eyes became glued to the screen as a soldier with a sub-machine gun mowed down wave upon wave of the enemy without once re-loading. The massacre finally came to an end.

'I know who else would love it here,' said Elsie with a gurgle of laughter.

'So do I,' said Sarah laying another garment on the ironing-board.

Mr Godfrey glanced up again in time to see the two girls exchange knowing looks. A private joke, he thought. Later there were some whispered consultations, but he didn't take much notice. He was too concerned about the impending visit to the bunker of the engineer. According to the entries in the logbook in the office at the entrance, he called every fourth week on a Thursday. He was due in two days' time. But six months ago he'd called on a Wednesday—unless the date of the entry had been a mistake. Suppose he changed his schedule again and turned up tomorrow and caught them there? Well, it was no use worrying about it.

Mr Godfrey prepared a check list. There mustn't be the slightest indication of their existence. The man would only be interested in the heating and lighting, the air-conditioning and whether the place had been broken into. He wouldn't check the food, for example. Wouldn't be able to, in fact. Three months supplies for fifty people occupied several storerooms. It would be some time before what they ate made any noticeable inroad on the stocks. On the other hand something quite trivial—a dirty cup in the sink, a made-up bed—would attract the man's attention immediately. He was accustomed to coming in month after month and finding everything exactly the same. Mr Godfrey went painstakingly over every item, determined not to miss anything that would give them away. They would quit the bunker for the whole day, taking all their things with them and leaving it just as they had found it. They'd have to take a chance on him climbing the rungs in the escape shaft to inspect the fastening on the cover at the top. It was most unlikely that he would do that. More than likely he was unaware of its existence.

'What about the electricity we've used? Won't it register on the meter?' Martin asked.

'The small amount we've used with lights and television is a drop in the ocean compared with what those heaters are using and they're on all the time. And when the engineer powers up the Plant-Room he'll gobble thousands of units. No one will notice our little bit extra.'

Mr Godfrey had assumed they would all spend the day together. He'd had it in mind to take in a Museum or two in London: the Science or the Natural History maybe. He was disconcerted when they were discussing it the night before and Martin said politely:

'We'd like a day on our own, if you don't mind. Perhaps we'll go and visit Dad.'

Mr Godfrey hid his disappointment. They had a right to assert their independence and it was a reminder to him that they had backgrounds of their own of which he knew little. He would content himself with a long hike over the Berkshire Downs.

In the morning, as they left, he tried to press money upon Martin for the fares.

'No, it's all right, thank you,' the boy insisted. 'We still have a little money of our own.'

It was then that an unhappy thought occurred to Mr Godfrey. They had all their gear with them, in the haversacks. . . .

'You are—' He faltered. 'You are coming back, aren't you?'

Martin gazed at him in surprise. 'Yes, of course.'

Elsie reached up and pecked his cheek. ''Bye, Arnold.'

Sarah said, in her breathless voice, 'See you tonight then.'

He felt very much alone as he toured the bunker making a final check.

Eight

Mr Godfrey approached the site cautiously on his return that evening. There was no sign of the white car he'd seen arrive in the morning when he remained behind to make sure that the engineer was, in fact, making a visit that day. Hidden from view, he had watched the car come slowly along the rough track in the woods and stop at the high, barred gates to the compound. A man got out and unfastened the padlock and chains, drove the car inside and refastened them. He followed the track on foot as it sloped down out of sight to the entrance doors to the bunker.

Arnold Godfrey had enjoyed his long walk on the Berkshire Downs along the ancient Ridgeway from Goring to Wantage, despite a chill wind and a steady drizzle. He was learning to live each day as it came and not to think of the past or of the future, though it bothered him a little that when he tried to remember the recent past his memory tended to cloud over. He knew he was running away from things but he couldn't recall the details. His memory simply seized up when it encountered anything unpleasant and he didn't attempt to unblock it.

He could remember a long way back very well and, if he wanted to, he could easily recall the War. A big, blonde Waaf corporal he'd met, for instance, when he was still an aircraftsman second class. He chuckled aloud, thinking of those lusty, love-making sessions on the river bank at Bedford. That strapping girl had been the young Mrs Godfrey before he married her. She'd been so full of zest . . . so enthusiastic. So had he . . . so had he. His laughter quickly died. All that eagerness, all that *feeling* . . . where had it gone?

The War had ended and a year later she'd had one of those women's operations—a hysterectomy, or something. Afterwards she'd lost interest in sex; and then she'd turned against it altogether. He would have liked to adopt a child but she wouldn't hear of it. When you came down to it, he thought, everything faded and died in the end. Youth, love, people—even memories—they always faded eventually. Unhappiness seemed the only thing that was constant.

He wasn't unhappy at the moment, though. Martin was a good lad, keen to learn and determined to make a success of his life. And Sarah, she was a nice girl, a continual reminder, with her quiet voice and serious manner, of Chick Courtney and his boyhood. As for Elsie, well, you couldn't tell how she'd turn out yet, but she was a friendly, cheerful little soul. Mr Godfrey sighed happily, looking upon them as his own children and seeing contentment stretching into the weeks ahead.

He neared the escape shaft and was pleased to see how well-camouflaged it was now. Since they arrived at Warren Row they'd tried to encourage the growth of foliage and grass around it. In the spring he would train the new growth over the concrete protrusion and hide it completely.

He'd arranged a signal with the children when they left that morning. Two sticks placed in a × beside the lid of the shaft meant *Stay Out*. If it was all clear to enter the sticks would be arranged in a T. He was put out to discover that the signal had been set in a T. That meant

71

the children were already inside. He had not intended them to return so early, nor to enter until he himself had checked that it was safe to do so. Still, they were back and that was a relief to him. He descended the shaft.

He stepped through the second of the airlock doors and went towards the kitchen where he could hear them talking. They were seated around the table eating. His eyes registered something different about them, but it was a moment before his brain took in what it was. He ran his eyes quickly over them again. There was *one head too many*. He moved round the table and stared at the new face. It belonged to a small boy about three years old with fair, curly hair. He was busily picking his nose and eating at the same time.

'Who's this?'

It was Elsie who answered. 'That's Darren,' she said. Then, adding the kind of irrelevant information that children of her age thought important, 'He's three and a half.'

'Where's he come from and what's he doing here?'

Sarah answered this time, delivering what sounded like a prepared statement. 'He lives in the flat below where we used to live. We often looked after him because his mum was on the drink and his stepfather beat him all the time. The other night we had a Family Conference and decided to rescue him. Up in London today we went back to the old place and asked around the kids in the neighbourhood to see if things had changed. They haven't—they're worse than ever for Darren. So we brought him away with us.' The speech over, she took a deep breath.

Mr Godfrey stared at her, wordless.

'We love Darren,' said Elsie, as though that explained everything.

He found his voice and babbled: 'You must take him back—take him back at once!'

'We can't,' said Martin.

'What do you mean, you can't?' The awful truth hit Mr Godfrey. 'You took him without permission!' he said accusingly.

Sarah said: 'There was no one to ask. It was midday and he was sitting on the floor in his pyjamas in a cold room, locked in and all alone. He was filthy dirty and—'

'Never mind all that!' His voice rose angrily. 'It's child-stealing—kidnapping! That's what it is!'

'No t'isn't!' Elsie piped up. 'He *wanted* to come with us, didn't you Darren?'

Darren, chomping away on a hunk of bread and jam, paused and nodded his head vigorously. He assessed Mr Godfrey slyly from the corner of his eyes. 'I love you,' he said without any warmth in his tone, and went on chewing.

'He says that when he's worried,' Sarah explained. 'Sometimes it saves him from a thrashing, you see.'

Mr Godfrey sensed big trouble. He felt no sympathy or affection for the blue-eyed little monster who threatened their secure, cosy lives. He shook his head helplessly and appealed to Martin.

'Martin, surely *you* can see that this is quite impossible?'

'There's nothing to worry about,' Martin replied. 'We weren't seen taking him and no one knows where he is. Anyway, I agreed to this and, if anything happens, I'll take full responsibility.'

Mr Godfrey gazed at him open-mouthed. '*You'll* take responsibility?' A sixteen-year-old. Or was he fifteen? He couldn't remember. '*You'll* take responsibility?' he repeated feebly. 'How can you?'

'Because we did it, not you—it's nothing to do with you—and I'm the eldest,' Martin told him.

Mr Godfrey stared at each of them in turn. 'You're mad!' he declared. 'You're all mad!'

Sarah went to the sink and filled the electric kettle. 'Why don't you sit down and have a nice cup of tea,

Arnold?' It was the first time she had used his christian name. 'Then I'll get you something to eat. You must be very hungry.'

Weakly, he threw up his hands. 'Mad,' he repeated, 'quite mad.'

'Now come along,' Sarah said briskly. 'What would you like for your supper, h'm? I bought some new-laid eggs today. Would you like two boiled eggs?'

He stared at her vacantly. He was trying to concentrate his mind on police enquiries . . . television news . . . but the thoughts wouldn't come and the images faded. Sarah laid a hand gently on his arm. 'With toast? I'll cut the toast into soldiers for you, like Darren has it. You'll like that.'

She spoke to him as though he were a child. He didn't mind. It was comforting.

He was awakened in the morning by a hand pulling aside the bedclothes.

'I love you,' said Darren trying to clamber in beside him.

'Well, I don't love you!' Mr Godfrey retorted, pushing him away and tucking the blanket tightly under his chin.

Darren's face set in a scowl. 'I love you!' he repeated in a louder voice, tugging at the blanket with grim determination.

'Go away!' cried Mr Godfrey.

He'd gone to bed early because he felt rotten. His clothes were damp when he undressed and he realised he should have worn better weatherproof clothing on his hike across the Downs. Now, with a muzzy head and a chest like lead, he recognised the onset of a heavy cold, if not something worse.

Darren scrambled on to the bed and bounced up and down on top of him, making his head throb. He sat up and lifted him off the bed. Immediately, Darren tried to climb up again. Mr Godfrey reached out and grabbed his shoulders to restrain him. He was astonished and a trifle alarmed at the ferocity of the boy's struggles. It was all he could do to keep hold of him. Then suddenly, before he realised what was happening, Darren lowered his head and bit him hard on the thumb. In an automatic reflex action he cuffed the boy sharply on the ear.

Darren at once let out a noisy howl and ran to the side of the cubicle. Mr Godfrey watched in amazement as he knelt by the hardboard partition and began pounding his head violently against it, making loud booming sounds. Sarah came running in.

'Darren!' She pulled the boy up and cuddled him tightly against her. The ritual head movements continued against her thigh for a moment or two and then ceased.

'He bit me,' Mr Godfrey said defensively.

'He's a very disturbed child,' said Sarah. She sounded like a social worker. 'We're used to his ways, you see. You mustn't mind because he can't help himself, poor little chap.'

Darren was glaring murderously from under her arm. 'I hate you!' he shouted at Mr Godfrey. 'I'll kill you!'

Sarah rocked him. 'Shh! Shh!'

'I think he actually means it,' Mr Godfrey said nervously.

'Why do you say that?' she asked quickly. There was an odd expression on her face. 'He hasn't . . .' she hesitated, 'he hasn't done anything else, has he?'

'No, he just seems very overwrought, that's all.' His throat was raw and his voice was a croak.

'You sound *awful*.'

'I feel pretty bad,' he admitted. 'I think I'll stay in bed. I'm afraid I must have caught a chill yesterday.'

'Oh, you poor man, I am sorry,' said Sarah sympathetically. 'Can I get you anything?'

'Just some aspirin from the medicine cabinet in the First Aid Room and a glass of water, please.'

When she returned he asked: 'Was there . . .? Is there anything on the news about Darren?'

'We haven't listened,' she said lightly. 'There's nothing to worry about. No one could possibly trace him here! She held out the glass of water to him..In the palm of her other hand were three asprin tablets. 'Now come along Arnold. Take your medicine and have a good sleep.'

He swallowed the tablets and fell back weakly. 'Please promise to wake me for the news later, Sarah.'

She regarded him doubtfully. 'It will only worry you if there is anything.'

'Please, I must know what's happening,' he insisted.

'All right, if you must,' she sighed.

He dozed off into a series of vivid dreams which kept him tossing and turning. Then a nightmare developed in which an immensely strong Darren chased all of them around the bunker brandishing a huge axe. He caught them one by one, beheading each victim with a great shout of joy until only Mr Godfrey was left. Finally he too was caught. Darren stood over him as he lay on the floor. 'I'll kill you! I'll kill you!' he shouted triumphantly. Then he began hacking Mr Godfrey's head off with the axe.

He awoke with a start and found Sarah tapping him on the shoulder.

'The news will be on in a moment,' she told him. 'I'm going to give Darren his bath because I don't think he ought to watch in case there is anything about him in the news. He understands a lot more than we think.'

Feeling as weak as a kitten Mr Godfrey rose stiffly and putting an overcoat over his pyjamas he tottered along to the Recreation Room where Elsie and Martin were sitting in front of the television.

It was in the news, of course. A full-scale hunt. Three-year-old boys—even little monsters like Darren—didn't disappear without there being a lot of fuss. Police frogmen were dragging the local ponds and canals as all the usual procedures in a missing child case were put into operation. There was no clue as to what had happened to little Darren, said the report in an ominous tone, but foul play could not be ruled out. A picture of an angelic-faced Darren appeared on the screen, his golden curls and blue eyes calculated to wring the heart of every watching mother.

Elsie was pop-eyed. This beat all her war films. 'There's Darren!' she cried. 'Isn't it exciting?' Arnold Godfrey gave her a sour look.

'They haven't the least idea where he is,' Martin observed with satisfaction.

'His mother and father will be very upset,' said Mr Godfrey.

'Stepfather,' Martin corrected. 'You needn't waste sympathy on them. They made Darren's life Hell!'

'In that case the police might suspect them of murdering him,' Mr Godfrey pointed out.

'Good! Serves them right!'

Mr Godfrey sighed. His head was swimming and he suffered bouts of shivering. He felt in no condition to argue.

On the way back to his cubicle he passed the kitchen. Sarah was bathing Darren in the sink. He was standing up clutching her round the neck and trying to rub himself against her.

Even the effort of walking had made Mr Godfrey breathless. 'I'm going back to bed, Sarah,' he said hoarsely.

She half-turned. 'Can I bring you anything?'

'A hot drink would be nice, thank you.'

Darren had jumped up and wrapped his legs round Sarah. Mr Godfrey was turning away when he saw that Darren's backside, now in full view, was not rosy-cheeked but a greyish-blue colour.

'What are those bruises on his bottom?'

Sarah disentangled the boy and stood him back in the

sink. 'That's where his stepfather beats him,' she said casually. 'He canes Darren most nights when he gets home from the pub.'

'What on earth for?'

She shrugged. 'He's that sort of man, I suppose.'

'Does no one do anything about it?'

She turned to him full face and looked at him curiously. 'You don't know much about things, do you, Arnold? What do you expect? Some fairy-godmother of a social worker to wave a magic wand and make everything come right? What would *you* do?'

'Well, for a start, I'd remove the child and—' He stopped.

She nodded. 'That's right. You'd take him away. Only *you'd* put him in a Home,' she ended scornfully.

'You've made your point, Sarah,' he muttered. He walked slowly back to his room, pausing for breath every now and again.

Later, when she brought him the hot drink, he said: 'It doesn't make it right, you know, taking Darren away like this.' He was shivering violently.

'Shh,' she said soothingly. She put a hand to his burning forehead. 'You're not to *worry*. You just lie there and get better. We'll look after you. It will be Christmas soon and you *must* get well for Christmas.'

Nine

The house surgeon in the Reading hospital hadn't intended to ruin Butch Fearon's Christmas. He was flying to Tangier that evening to spend Christmas and the New Year in the sun and, looking through his case notes, he'd decided to bring forward those ward visits which would otherwise have had to await his return. In the rush to complete the cases, and because of a too hasty glance at his notes, he mistakenly assumed that Butch already understood the nature and consequences of his injuries.

The surgeon's schedule depended on spending not more than two minutes, on average, at each bedside. He galloped through his opening remarks to Butch Fearon.

'. . . lucky that the damage was localised . . . other pleasures in life besides sex, of course . . .' He looked up with a reassuring smile and concluded with brief, routine comments. '. . . bandages off tomorrow then, old chap. Happy Christmas!'

He was turning to the next bed when his patient, who until then had been staring at him, transfixed, came upright in the bed and seized his wrist.

In a whisper quivering with utter disbelief Butch asked:

'You mean, doc, *I'll never be able to screw again?*'

The doctor freed himself. 'I'm sorry, I thought you already understood that, Mr Fearon.' Wordlessly, Butch shook his head. 'Must be quite a nasty shock then, old chap. Try not to dwell on it too much. We'll give you something to calm you down.'

He patted Butch's arm and moved along with his retinue, muttering an instruction to one of the nurses. He'd left the ward before a full realisation flooded into his patient's mind.

Butch Fearon began cursing. The words came slowly at first, and in a normal voice. Then on a rising note and with increasing viciousness a torrent of swearing and threats poured from him. The nurses had some difficulty in forcing the Valium tablets down him and it was some time before the ward became peaceful again.

In the underground bunker at Warren Row Mr Godfrey was awakened very early on Christmas morning by an unusual buzzing sound. The fever which had laid him up for several days had left him and he felt normal again. The buzzing sound was repeated and he tried to place it. The overhead lights were on and the electric wall clock showed 0500. He yawned. Five o'clock in the morning was no time for rising. He closed his eyes again. A moment later he heard whispering and then Elsie's voice close by his ear.

'Are you awake, Arnold?'

He opened one eye. She stood by his bed in her nightie. He opened the other eye and sat up.

'He's awake!' she shouted. Sarah and Darren appeared in the doorway in pyjamas. The buzzer sounded again. 'What's that noise?' he asked.

'That's Martin's Christmas surprise for you,' Sarah told him. 'He's rigged up an alarm so that if anyone opens the entrance doors a warning buzzer sounds down here. He's used the lighting circuit and hidden the buzzer inside a light fitting.'

'That's very clever of him,' said Mr Godfrey, 'but why is the alarm sounding now?'

'Oh, that's just to demonstrate it. He's up at the entrance working the contact with his finger.'

He peered at the clock to make sure he hadn't mistaken the hour. 'But it's five o'clock in the morning.'

'It's *Christmas!*' chorussed Sarah and Elsie.

'I love you,' said Darren to no one in particular.

'We can't wait to open our presents,' Elsie said. 'Come on!'

Slightly dazed, he pulled an overcoat on over his pyjamas and followed them. In the Recreation Room, in the corner by the television, stood a Christmas tree. It was decorated with coloured paper and underneath it on the floor were several small parcels in Christmas wrapping paper.

'Isn't it a beauty? Martin dug it up on the far side of the wood,' Sarah said proudly.

'And I helped him put it in a bucket of earth,' said Elsie.

'*I* widdled in the bucket,' Darren announced.

'Yes, you made it *smell!*' Elsie scolded.

'We're going to have a proper Christmas,' Sarah said. 'A Christmas tree, presents, turkey, Christmas pudding —it's going to be fun!'

Mr Godfrey was about to ask where the money for all these things had come from, but he thought better of it. He wondered if they'd helped themselves to some of his money while he lay ill in bed, and then dismissed the thought. They wouldn't do that, he was sure.

Martin joined them and they opened their presents. There was one for each of them.

'Martin chose the presents for Elsie, Darren and me,' Sarah explained to Mr Godfrey, 'and I chose yours.'

Sarah had a book on wildflowers. Martin had an electronic calculator. Elsie's present was a set of soldiers in battledress armed with commando knives and sub-machine guns; and Darren had an Action Man. Un-wrapping his own gift, Mr Godfrey found it was a bottle of whisky.

'It was the most expensive we could find,' Sarah told him as he studied the label. 'You do like it, don't you,' she asked anxiously.

'Oh yes, thank you. It is an excellent whisky. But you shouldn't have spent your money like this.'

'Oh, we didn't. We've hardly any money of our own left. We went out and collected some.'

'Collected?'

'Yes. I put on my old Guide uniform and Elsie wore her Brownie outfit and we took the bus into Reading and went from house-to-house with a collecting box. We told people we were collecting for poor children . . . to give them a good Christmas.'

'But that was dishonest!' he protested.

'I don't think so,' Sarah said calmly. 'We didn't tell any lies. The money was for poor children for Christmas.'

'Yes, *us!*' Elsie burbled with laughter.

The day passed like a dream for Mr Godfrey. They did indeed have turkey and Christmas pudding. The turkey had been cooked with the giblets still inside in their plastic bag.

'I thought that was the stuffing,' Sarah explained. 'I thought turkeys were ready-stuffed when you bought them.' But the taste wasn't affected so no one minded.

They wore funny hats and became very merry over Christmas dinner, partly on account of drinking a lot of red wine.

'We must have wine with our dinner,' Martin insisted. 'I bought it specially.'

Even Elsie and Darren were given wine. Mr Godfrey didn't approve but he said nothing. Darren spat his out after the first mouthful but Elsie swigged her ration with gusto, maintaining 'it's delicious'. During the meal she put away another glassful and emptied Darren's glass as well, apparently with no effect.

Afterwards, as Mr Godfrey sat in an armchair feeling somnolent, Darren climbed on to his lap.

'Are you my Daddy now?' he lisped.

'No, I'm not!'

'I love you.'

'Er—yes,' said Mr Godfrey warily, as Darren's arms encircled his neck.

'He's jus' like baby Jesus,' Elsie declared from a prone position on the floor. The wine had got to her at last and she was lying flat on her back, glassy-eyed.

Sarah said softly: 'There, you see, Darren likes you really.'

Mr Godfrey nodded peacefully. The arms seemed to be tightening around his neck but he was too drowsy to care. He felt Sarah gently remove the boy from his lap.

'Happy Christmas, Arnold.' Her lips brushed his forehead.

'Happy Christmas, Sarah,' he mumbled, dozing off.

'Happy Christmas, Dena.'

Earlier that morning, in a fashionable house overlooking Regent's Park and in front of a larger and more heavily decorated tree than the one in the underground bunker at Warren Row, a girl about the same age as Sarah smiled happily as her father handed her his present. Usually she knew in advance what it would be because he always bought her the most expensive item on her Christmas List. But this year she had included in the List—along with 'perfume', 'typewriter' and 'leather boots'—the words *solid gold bracelet*. From the moment she awoke that morning Dena had been sick with excitement wondering if she would receive the present she wanted. If she did, if he really *had* bought her a gold bracelet the girls at school would be wild with jealousy. They'd be pop-eyed!

Saul Harrison smiled indulgently as his daughter tore eagerly at the wrapping-paper. She opened the costly, padded box and gave a shriek of delight.

'Daddy! Oh, Daddy, you *darling*!' She threw her arms round his neck and kissed him extravagantly on the mouth.

Over her shoulder Harrison caught a look from his wife, Louise. He frowned. Hell! He'd bought *her* a real fur coat. She had no damned right to look at him like that! Deliberately, he muzzled Dena's hair with his face, his own fair, curly hair contrasting sharply with his daughter's dark tresses. He knew it annoyed his wife when he spoiled Dena or paid her too much attention. Saul Harrison was used to having his own way, whether it was in business dealings or in bed with a woman and it irked him that he'd never quite mastered Louise. Those cool, grey eyes of hers forever kept him at a distance. Sometimes, as now, he was goaded into getting his own back through their daughter.

'When you two have finished petting, we'll have coffee,' his wife said tartly.

Gently he disengaged Dena and picked up the last of his Christmas mail from the mantelpiece. His wife had already opened the 'Mr & Mrs' correspondence and the Christmas cards. The three envelopes remaining were addressed to him and he'd been too busy to look at them until now. The first two contained bills. Saul picked up the third envelope. He slit it open, took out the single sheet of paper and unfolded it. There were just twelve words typed in capitals:

IS SARAH HAVING A NICE CHRISTMAS? DOES YOUR WIFE KNOW ABOUT HER?

Saul went pale. Keeping his back to his wife and daughter he folded the sheet with hands that shook slightly and replaced it in the envelope.

Arnold Godfrey shifted restlessly in the armchair, his contented post-Christmas dinner snooze ruffled by images and visions. He was unused to large meals and rich food or to swamping his stomach with wine. His digestive system was sending out signals of distress and his brain, to protect his sleep, was craftily converting the signals to dream sequences.

The present dream had started pleasantly enough with him telling his chief in the council offices exactly what he thought of the council for making him redundant. Mr Godfrey had been producing the annual Register of Electors for the Borough for many, many years. It was a job he enjoyed with its set procedures and its unvarying timetable each year. He took a pride in the work and in its usefulness and he liked the importance that people attached to it at the time of elections. Then, of a sudden, some bright-eyed computer consultant had designed a computer system, specified the equipment and before Mr Godfrey realised what was happening his work was being performed by the latest 'word-processing' equipment and he was out of a job.

The action of his dream moved on and he was holding forth to the whole council, including the mayor, about their treachery. The images faded and his dreams jumped back some thirty years to wartime. It was the occasion when during their engagement Mrs Godfrey—or Monica Brooks as she was then—took him home to Pontefract to meet her family. In his dream he relived two memories of that visit. One was of going to a dance with Monica that started at midnight and finished at four o'clock in the morning—something that was quite normal in the mining community of Pontefract. The RAF had conditioned him to being in camp at midnight—by that magic deadline of 2359 hours. All service dances and social activities finished in time for that. Setting out for a dance at midnight and later pirouetting to the strains of the last waltz at dawn

85

seemed to have a certain sinfulness about it. At any rate it added spice to their lovemaking under the sunrise on the way home.

The other memory was of sharing a double bed with Monica's two young brothers. Arnold was an only child and he'd never shared a bed with anyone before. He'd gone hot with embarrassment when the younger boy snuggled up to him and he'd quickly turned his back on him. In his dream now he again felt the boy's arms stealing round his neck. Then the dream became a nightmare as the arms tightened relentlessly and he began to choke.

He came suddenly awake and saw Sarah and Martin lying on the floor asleep. He tried to call out but his windpipe was being crushed and he could only make gulping noises. From behind, Darren's arms were wedged under Mr Godfrey's chin and folded across his throat in a hug of death. He staggered to his feet with Darren clinging to his back and his legs locked round Mr Godfrey's middle. Consciousness was slipping away fast as he plucked weakly at the boy's arms. In desperation he stamped a tattoo on the floor with his heels.

Sarah opened her eyes and looked up. He saw her eyes widen in alarm.

'*Darren!*' she shouted, scrambling to her feet.

There was no slackening of the throttling arms round Arnold Godfrey's neck and he sank, fainting, to his knees. Before he passed out he was dimly aware of Sarah calling:

'No, Darren. *Friend. Friend.*' She spoke the words as though she were giving a command.

It seemed an age later when he heard Elsie ask, matter-of-factly:

'Is he dead?'

He came to, lying on the floor, with Sarah kneeling beside him looking anxious. Her face flooded with relief as he sat up and gingerly rubbed his neck. The blood flowed through the carotid arteries to his brain once more and his head had cleared but he felt as though he'd suffered the attentions of a boa-constrictor.

'I'm sure Darren didn't mean anything,' Sarah said earnestly. 'He's just very strong and he doesn't under-stand that you mustn't hold people round their necks like that.'

She stood up and pulled the boy forward by the hand. 'Now, Darren, say sorry to Arnold for frightening him like that!'

Darren nodded and grinned, baring his even little teeth like a dog. 'Sorry,' he said. 'I love Arnold. Arnold's my friend.'

Mr Godfrey looked at him grimly. He'd come very close to death and it didn't matter whether Darren knew what he was doing or not. He'd still have been dead if Sarah hadn't come to his aid.

'Where on earth did he learn to do a thing like that?'

Sarah looked uncomfortable. Darren had had an odd association with an older boy, a teenager, who worked at a kennels where they trained guard dogs. The boy had thought it amusing to train Darren like a dog. He'd chosen his pupil only too well. On the command 'Kill! Kill!' Darren would leap on to his victim's back and start throttling him. The call-off command was 'Friend! Friend!' The bizarre business had come to light when Darren had almost killed a playmate, although on that occasion no one had called 'Kill! Kill!' Darren had simply been feeling anti-social.

Sarah didn't think it would help to explain this to Mr Godfrey. 'It was a silly game he learned,' she muttered. 'I thought he'd forgotten it.'

'I suppose I should be thankful he didn't attack me while I was lying ill and helpless in bed.'

'Oh, we kept him out of your room,' Sarah said

cheerfully. 'He was longing to come and see you but we wouldn't let him in.'

'He said he wanted to watch you dying,' Elsie explained helpfully.

Ten

Saul Harrison hated the week after Christmas. He'd always hated it even as a child. There was a sadness about it, a sense of let-down after the long build-up to the two or three magic days of Christmas.

Now, as he drove along a decaying back-street in Hackney looking for a place to put the car, his gloom deepened. This had been a rather nice part of London when he'd last known it twelve or thirteen years ago. He saw a vacant space at the kerb, pulled into it and parked the car. A Daimler would be conspicuous in this area and he didn't want to drive right up to the address in it. He wasn't sure how he was going to handle the situation but there was no point in drawing attention to the difference between his own comfortable circumstances and those of the family he was about to confront.

He locked the Daimler and walked along the street, briskly at first then slowing as he became less certain of his surroundings. He knew the house he was looking for and the number of it—he could remember that. But whole stretches of the street had been torn down to make way for blocks of flats and he realised that the address was farther along than he had thought. Saul Harrison plodded on. Once he would have hurried eagerly along this street. Hurried from the place where he'd discreetly parked his little MG sports. Even then he used to park away from the house—but that was so the neighbours wouldn't gossip.

His affair with Sarah's mother had been passionate, but brief. It had lasted only three months. He'd met Carol Pace in Eastbourne while he was attending a conference at the Congress Hall there. In those days he was striving to make his way in the cut-throat world of micro-electronics. A few months earlier he'd married Louise. Her father was chairman of a Finance House and Saul was receiving a lot of help from him in providing capital for his new business. That hadn't been Saul's only reason for marrying Louise. She was beautiful and clever and he wanted to possess this dark, willowy girl. But it had been a powerful incentive that, through her, he could lay hands on the capital he needed.

The money had been forthcoming all right; but Louise proved to be a big disappointment. This alluring creature, to whom he'd so readily tied himself, regarded sex as something to be endured—like a manicure or a beauty facial, but a good deal less frequently, if possible. Sex was not an act of pleasure to be enjoyed. Her coolness in bed enraged Saul and injured his pride. And she could deploy a range of emasculating remarks.

LOUISE (tired voice): 'Not now, darling, I *couldn't*. My tummy's upset.

LOUISE (drawling): 'You don't expect me to open my legs *every* time you ask surely?'

LOUISE (cuttingly, usually after a row): 'Daddy's lent you *oodles* of money. Why can't you be satisfied with that?'

Carol Pace was a different kind of girl altogether. She was warm and uncomplicated and she had a soft, gentle nature. Her hair was golden and she had a permanent high colour that made her look as though she was constantly blushing. She was staying in the same guest-house as Saul, in the less fashionable end of Eastbourne, near the Redoubt. She was on holiday with her small son, a ginger-haired boy called Martin. Her husband was in the army overseas—or so she told Saul. Later he found out that Joseph Pace was actually on remand in Brixton prison, awaiting trial on a burglary charge. As far as Saul could make out it was not the first time that Joseph Pace had helped himself to other people's property. Carol hadn't known this when she married him and she was bewildered by it. She was young—barely twenty—alone and vulnerable. She was defenceless against Saul Harrison's charm.

The conference lasted a week and every night after the other guests had retired he left his room on the first floor and mounted the stairs to Carol's attic-bedroom at the top of the house. Ever after, when he heard the sounds of the sea swishing pebbles back and forth on a beach it reminded him of that little room with its dormer window facing the sea. He remembered how Carol used to make quick yelping noises like a puppy when she climaxed. Sometimes it woke the sleeping child in the cot beside them. Then she would reach out and, with Saul still deep inside her, soothe the boy to sleep again.

Saul was infatuated with the girl and when the week was over and they both returned to London he continued the affair. He was overjoyed, without any feeling of guilt, when her husband received a six-month prison sentence. The Paces had a ground-floor flat in a terrace house in Hackney. Saul contrived to spend one or two evenings a week with Carol and even the occasional night without raising Louise's suspicions. Louise might not be interested in sex with him herself but he was certain she would be truly vicious if she discovered he was having an affair with someone else.

Then, three months after they'd met, Carol told him she was pregnant. In a panic Saul saw himself losing Louise, losing the support of his father-in-law's money, and the collapse of his business. His infatuation with Carol died instantly. Instinctively, he tried to buy his way out of trouble.

'You won't have a thing to worry about,' he told Carol confidently. 'I'll pay for an abortion.'

'*You'll what?*' Carol's voice was filled with horror.

'Well, you can't very well have it, can you?' he asked reasonably. 'I mean what did you expect?'

'*Expect?* I expected you to stand by me. I—I thought you loved me. I thought we would—' She faltered and burst into tears.

Saul felt trapped. Angrily, he listed all the reasons why she shouldn't have the baby. It would wreck their lives— hers in particular. Surely she could see that? Her husband . . . he'd go berserk, wouldn't he?

'There he is, stuck in prison—and he finds out his wife's having a baby by another man. He'd kill you. He'd—'

'He's not that sort of man,' Carol said wearily. 'Joe is very gentle and easy-going. Anyway I was going to divorce him. Divorce is easy when your husband's in prison. I've seen a solicitor. Joe would agree to it, I know.'

Saul was startled. He hadn't realised she'd thought things through that far. This wasn't what he wanted at all. The consequences looked even worse than he'd feared and he began to argue more stridently. The longer he argued, the more distraught Carol became. The quarrel grew ugly and bitter.

His last memory of that parting scene was of Carol standing in the hallway of the flat, her eyes shining fiercely. It was a Carol he didn't know, a steely-voiced girl stripping away his excuses and leaving him bare and undignified.

'You know what the problem is, Saul? It's *you!* *You're* the problem. Not me . . . not the baby . . . not my husband. *You!* You've no guts!'

He stood mute, letting her words wash over him. Carol continued:

'Don't come here again and don't write to me. Just go away and stay away. Thank God there's still time to convince Joe the baby's his.' She smiled sadly. 'We were sleeping together right up to the night he was arrested. He won't even question it if I tell him we're having another baby.'

Saul saw a hope of deliverance. Here was the answer—the perfect answer. Overcome with relief he said quickly:

'You must let me help financially.'

She rounded on him. 'I don't want your money, damn you! And don't ever send any or I'll post it straight back to your wife!'

He shivered. She knew where he lived, of course. He'd forgotten that.

Carol saw his expression and her lip curled. 'Don't worry, she'll not hear from me otherwise.'

He'd turned away then, ready to leave. Anxious to be free.

'But I promise you one thing, Saul.' Her words stopped him at the door. What now?

'I'll never let you forget that you have a child. No one else will know . . . but you and I will. Every year I'll remind you. Every year on its birthday . . . wherever you are. You can depend on it!'

He relaxed again. Was that all? It didn't sound very serious. Anyway, she'd probably drop the idea when she'd calmed down. Thankfully, he escaped.

Over the next few weeks he tried harder with Louise, partly because he felt guilty but more because parting from Carol had left him with a deep physical longing. He was kinder to Louise and the three month affair with Carol had made him a better lover. Louise became less brittle, less aloof. A few months later she too became pregnant.

To Saul's surprise she revelled in her new state. She'd always been so concerned with her figure and her clothes and her appearance that he'd expected her to be annoyed; but she was positively aglow with satisfaction and during those months before the baby arrived Saul was happy. Even the arrival of a card from Carol didn't mar his happiness.

Mr and Mrs Joseph Pace are pleased to announce the birth of a daughter Sarah on 27th July. A sister for Martin.

The envelope was addressed to him but, in any case, there had been no risk of Louise opening it. She was fanatical about privacy—other people's as well as her own—and she would never have dreamed of opening his letters.

So, Carol was carrying out her threat. Well, he didn't care; and he found the thought of being a father twice over was rather a pleasant one.

Louise had a difficult time giving birth to Dena. Her small hips and narrow pelvis were not designed for easy childbirth. Afterwards she made it clear to Saul that she had no intention of going through the experience again. Once more her attitude to sex became decidedly cool.

On 27th July the following year the first photograph of Sarah arrived. There was no accompanying letter but written on the reverse were the words: *Sarah, aged one year*. The photograph annoyed Saul whereas the card the previous year had not done so. The thought of another child—his child—was bearable; but visual evidence in the form of a photo turned thought into reality. That, he didn't like. He shut away thought and reality quickly, locking the photograph in his deed box with the card from the year before.

From then on, every year on Sarah's birthday, or within a day or so after, he received a photo. *Sarah, aged two. Sarah aged three. Sarah. . . .* The annual repetition irritated

Saul. Carol and Sarah seemed like ghostly shadows that could flit into his life at any time and upset his settled existence. His business had developed successfully; his marriage was tolerable. True, he resorted to call-girls and there were one-night stands with the wives of business associates; but he regarded his life as settled. He disliked Carol's disturbing reminders from the past.

Then the photographs stopped. In the year in which he should have received one inscribed: *Sarah, aged five*, nothing came. At first Saul thought it might have been delayed in the post, or gone astray. Then after several weeks had passed he wondered if Carol had at last dropped the annual ritual. Somehow he doubted that. *I'll never let you forget . . . every year . . . wherever you are. . . .* No, that wouldn't be the explanation. Maybe she'd remarried; or the child had died. Or perhaps, after all, he'd receive another picture of her next year. *Sarah, aged six.*

Saul was a man who couldn't bear uncertainty. He had to find out the answer. He telephoned an enquiry agent and was put out to discover that, despite offering a high fee, he couldn't have the matter handled at arm's length. The man refused to accept instructions over the telephone and Saul had to go and see him, since he didn't want the man calling at his home.

'I simply want you to find out what's happened to this woman and to her child. Find out where they . . . if they're all right. That's simple enough, isn't it? I've given you the address to start from. You don't need to know anything more.'

'Oh, but we do, sir. We need to know what we might be getting ourselves into.' Saul resented the man's manner and his use of 'we', when it was obvious that he ran a one-man show. The man went on, 'Now, you seem respectable enough but . . .' The words hung in the air. Saul stared him down. Unabashed the man continued:

'Perhaps you wouldn't mind telling me your reasons for wanting to find—' he glanced down at his notes, '—Carol Pace and her little girl, Sarah?'

'I told you, it's none of your business!' Saul replied angrily. 'You sound like a damned policeman!'

'I expect that's because I used to be one before I retired, sir,' the man answered smugly. 'Look at it this way. You could be a father wanting to harass his ex-wife. A pervert after a—' He saw the flash of anger in Saul's eyes and added smoothly, '—anything.'

'If I had criminal intentions, I'd hardly employ an enquiry agent.'

'You might, you might.' The balding head wobbled on the hunched shoulders. 'But you *wouldn't* if everything was as simple as you say. After all, you could have been there and back in a taxi to this address in the time it's taken you to tell me about it. And for less than my fee will cost you. So there has to be more than you've told me, doesn't there?'

The watery blue eyes fastened on him. The whites of the eyes, in the corners, were an unhealthy, muddy colour. Saul disliked the man but, having gone this far, he didn't intend wasting further time on selecting someone else. Looking him straight in the face he said:

'I had an affair with Carol Pace some years ago. The child is mine. Every year Carol used to send me a photograph of Sarah. This year I haven't heard from her. I want to know if something is wrong.' He paused, trying to find the right words. 'I don't want to stir up the past . . . open old wounds. To—'

'To have them round your neck again?' The eyes were wet and knowing. 'I understand, sir. Quite natural. Thank you for being frank. It always helps, you know.' The man was insufferable. Saul would have liked to punch him in the face.

In spite of his dislike he was impressed with the

enquiry agent's speed and efficiency when, a week later, he received a neatly-typed, two-page report. Carol Pace, the report told him, had died in April of last year giving birth to her third child, Elsie. (Copy of death certificate, obtained from Registrar of Births and Deaths, attached.) The other subject of the enquiry, the report went on, Sarah, aged five years, was alive and healthy. So far as the agent could tell she was leading a normal, happy life. Account for fees and expenses was enclosed. Prompt settlement would be appreciated.

Saul was relieved. *No one else will know.* Those had been Carol's words. Now, only *he* knew about Sarah. There would be no more photos—no more fear that his secret would come out. Saul locked the report away in his deed box along with the photographs. That chapter of his life was finally closed.

Eight years had passed. Eight years during which Sarah's existence faded from his thoughts. He'd virtually forgotten her. All there was to her—all there'd ever been for him—were four photographs of a little girl with long, blonde hair and high-coloured cheeks like her mother.

Then, out of nowhere, had come that note. IS SARAH HAVING A NICE CHRISTMAS? DOES YOUR WIFE KNOW ABOUT HER? It seemed senseless, childish even. There was no demand for money. What was the idea? Just to spoil his Christmas? No, it was more sinister than that, he was sure. Someone was letting him know—putting him on warning that they knew his secret and he could expect to be bled.

Now, as Saul walked along the dreary street in Hackney and reached the address, he wondered if he had over-reacted. Wouldn't he have been wiser to leave things alone . . . to wait and see what happened? But, for Saul, it was the same situation as eight years ago when the photographs had suddenly stopped. He had to know why. He could have employed an enquiry agent again except that, this time, the circumstances were different. It wasn't a question of finding someone, but of finding out what they wanted. Money, presumably, although the note didn't make any demand. That meant negotiation. Saul intended to carry that out for himself.

He stood on the opposite side of the street, gazing at the house. When Carol had lived there it had been brightly-painted, neat and well-kept. Today the paint was peeling from the front door, the woodwork round the windows looked rotten and the whole building was run-down and neglected. He crossed the road and mounted the flight of steps leading to the front door. Of course, Joe Pace and the children might not live here now. Saul hesitated. Well, he had to start somewhere. He reached out and pressed the bell.

Eleven

In the underground bunker at Warren Row Mr Godfrey and the children were ending their morning lessons. It was at this period each day that they came together to discuss what they would do in the afternoon. Whether they would go on a nature ramble or a shopping expedition or perhaps play games if the weather was bad. Until this time Martin and Sarah would follow their own studies, referring to Mr Godfrey if they needed advice. He usually helped Elsie with her reading and writing and tried to keep Darren out of mischief.

Darren was undoubtedly a problem child and it had been agreed that keeping an eye on him was a full-time responsibility which should be shared fairly. Mr Godfrey wasn't sure that it was really fair for him to have to take a share since he hadn't wanted Darren in the first place. They all agreed what Darren's problems were. The question was, were they getting worse or better? Mr Godfrey could see no improvement in the little horror's behaviour and this morning he'd said so as Darren chased Elsie and tried to pull down her jeans.

'Oh, he's much better now,' Sarah insisted. 'He doesn't wet himself any more and he only bit Elsie twice last week.'

'He worms his way into her bed in the middle of the night and tries to mount her!'

'Yes . . . well, he's a bit of a nuisance like that. But he's only a *little* boy.'

Mr Godfrey snorted. Little he might be, but the boy was a homicidal maniac, a budding rapist and he had a mental age of fourteen in some things. 'How long do you propose to keep him?' he asked gloomily.

'Oh, for always,' she replied airily. 'All the fuss has died down. There hasn't been a mention on the television news for ages.'

'That doesn't mean the police have given up,' he warned her.

Suddenly there was a sound that made them all freeze.

'That's the alarm buzzer in your bedroom, Arnold,' Martin whispered. 'Someone has opened the entrance doors.'

Mr Godfrey took command. 'Quick! Leave everything and out through the escape shaft. Martin! Switch off the buzzer. Sarah! Lead the way and keep out of sight when you come out at the top.'

'Absolute quiet now,' he ordered as they moved off.

Darren's head swivelled round and his eyes crinkled in a wicked grin. Telling Darren to keep quiet was to invite immediate disobedience. His mouth opened on a deep breath as he prepared to howl defiance.

'*Sarah!*' Mr Godfrey called urgently in a low voice.

She looked down and promptly clamped a hand over Darren's mouth. He tried to bite her and she kneed him in the back and pushed him along in front of her, keeping a firm grip on his nose and mouth.

They emerged above ground and crouched in the thin, damp undergrowth. The high, barred gates to the compound stood open but there was no sign of life.

'Sarah, you stay here with Elsie and Darren while Martin and I move forward to see what's happening.'

She was still wrestling with Darren who was furious at being restrained and was struggling madly. She stooped, barely able to hold him as he threshed about on the ground. Elsie saw that he was about to break free and flung herself on top of him.

'Shut up and keep still you little bugger!' she cried fiercely, 'or we'll take you back to your mum!'

The effect was remarkable. Darren always seemed to puff up and grow bigger when he was angry. At Elsie's threat he shrank about three sizes and became limp and submissive. The girls released him and he sat sucking his thumb.

Martin and Mr Godfrey went towards the entrance to the compound, dodging from tree to tree. They couldn't see anyone beyond the open gates. Then there was the sound of an approaching engine and a dark-green heavy van appeared, rumbling along the track leading from the road. It turned in through the gates followed by a second and then a third vehicle.

Mr Godfrey studied the scene as the vans halted and men stepped out and began unloading them.

'Stores,' he told Martin after a while. 'Lots of stores. And equipment.'

'What for? What does it mean?'

'It means,' said Mr Godfrey grimly, 'that they're preparing for an exercise. *The headquarters is going to be activated.*'

'When? Now?'

'No, not now. Probably this week-end. The civil defence volunteers who man these exercises have to do their normal jobs during the week.'

'But you said this place wouldn't be used again. You said they'd stopped exercising.'

'They had. But haven't you been watching the news on TV? Haven't you noticed what's been happening in the world? The trouble between the Americans and the Russians?'

Martin shook his head. Mr Godfrey gazed at him sadly.

101

No, of course the boy wouldn't be interested in international crises. Why should he be? Mr Godfrey hadn't been when he was that age. That was in the Thirties. Would he have listened if anyone had tried to warn him what the coming war would mean to his generation? That he'd enter the war a boy and leave it a man; and that he'd never recover those lost years of adolescence? He doubted if he would have listened or understood. Sombrely he went on:

'The government has been threatening to call out the Civil Defence again. My guess is that they're about to test their contingency plans for Warren Row.'

He saw the puzzled look on the boy's face. 'Martin, what will happen is that a lot of men and women will pour into this headquarters and start rushing around pretending there has been a nuclear attack on London.'

'You mean, like army exercises?'

'Yes, that's it.'

'What about *us*? What shall we do?'

'I don't know. There's nothing we *can* do for the moment. When these men have left we'll return inside and hold a family council to decide what to do.'

'Won't they find our things and know that someone's been living down there?'

'I doubt it. These men are just suppliers and they'll be in and out of the storerooms, but nowhere else. If they did notice anything unusual they'd only think it was to do with the civil defence people.'

When they were assembled together in the bunker later Mr Godfrey began mournfully:

'We'll just have to collect everything up and leave. There's nothing else to be done.'

'But it's our *home*,' Elsie wailed. 'Why *should* we leave? You said we could stay here for ever and ever!'

He hadn't quite said that, but it was near enough true

and he felt that he'd let them down. That in some way it was his fault they would have to depart from here.

'Where could we go?' asked Sarah. 'It's winter and it's too cold for camping and I don't want to go back on the Tube.'

They were silent for a while, busy with their thoughts. Darren sat on the floor gnawing his thumb. He couldn't understand the discussion but he sensed the air of uncertainty.

'Why can't we *hide*?' Elsie demanded. 'Arnold says it will only be two or three days. Why don't we hide instead of leaving?'

'Don't be silly,' Sarah said crushingly. 'We couldn't.'

'I bet *I* could! In a cupboard or somewhere. They wouldn't find me and then, at night . . .' she warmed to the idea, 'I'd—I'd sneak out and steal my food . . . and then—'

'Could we *make* a hideout?' Martin interrupted. 'This is a big place. Surely we could find a corner somewhere—perhaps dig ourselves a hiding place?'

'Cut a new room—a secret room—out of the chalk, you mean?' Mr Godfrey combed thin fingers through his white hair and pursed his lips. 'Well, there are trenching tools and picks and shovels in the stores. It might just be possible, I suppose. But, five of us?' He stopped, seeing the snag. Elsie had temporarily lost interest in the problem and was attempting to stop Darren from chewing his thumb. Mr Godfrey leaned towards Martin and Sarah.

'What about . . . *you know who*?' He wasn't going to alert the little devil by saying his name. 'He'll never keep quiet and behave. He'll give us *all* away.' He saw his opportunity, seized it and went on persuasively: 'Now's the time to return him.' He met their eyes and saw that they understood. He delivered the ultimatum firmly:

'Darren must go. If not, I won't help you any further.'

Avoiding Sarah's eyes he spoke to Martin. 'All you

have to do is take him into Reading, pop into a phone box, dial 999 and leave him there. The police will do the rest. He'll be well taken care of.'

No one spoke for a moment or two. Then Sarah said:

'Elsie, take Darren walkies along the tunnel. Play horses with him. He likes that.'

Eagerly Darren began unhooking his belt as Elsie galloped off up the tunnel neighing like a horse. He ran after her in close pursuit, shrieking and flaying at her legs with his belt.

'He'll injure her!' Mr Godfrey cried in alarm.

'No he won't,' Sarah assured him. 'Elsie won't let him. She can manage him.'

She exchanged glances with Martin. He coughed and said:

'Arnold, there's something you don't know about Darren . . . something Elsie doesn't know either.'

'He's our brother,' Sarah said.

'*What?* How can he be?' Mr Godfrey gobbled with agitation.

'Mum died when Elsie was born, as I told you,' she said. 'So Dad was left with a baby to bring up as well as Martin and me. There was this lady living in the flat below us and she helped to look after we children. Dad and her became sort of . . . friendly. And—' Sarah hesitated and dropped her head. Her long hair fell over her face.

'And Dad put this woman in the club,' Martin said in a flat voice. 'Darren was the result. So, he's our brother, or half-brother actually.'

Mr Godfrey was defeated and bewildered. 'But you said he's ill-treated. You gave me a tale about his step-father beating him every night,' he said accusingly.

'It's *true*! I told you the truth!' Sarah insisted.

'You see, Dad broke it off with Jean—that's the woman's name—before Darren was born,' Martin explained, 'and he didn't let on to us that Darren was his until he went in prison. By then Jean had shacked up with a lorry driver. He knocks Hell out of her . . . and Darren. Jean's hopeless . . . always round the pub boozing and picking up men. Sarah often used to look after Darren— just to get him out of it. 'Course, we didn't dream he was really Dad's.'

'We couldn't let him go back to that.' Sarah's blue eyes appealed to Mr Godfrey.

'Why didn't you tell me this before?' he asked.

'Dad asked us not to tell anyone—not even Elsie.'

'She'd only blow it around,' Martin commented. 'And she'd be bound to tell Darren. If his stepfather found out he'd half-kill Jean. He's as jealous as Hell about her past with other men.'

Mr Godfrey shrugged his shoulders as the hope of being rid of Darren receded. 'Well, we can't stay here while the exercise is on. We can't hide ourselves with Darren around.'

'We'll keep him under control,' Martin promised.

'A big box or a small cupboard is what we need,' Sarah suggested. 'We'll shut him up if we have to.'

'He won't like that!' For all his ill-feeling to Darren Mr Godfrey was appalled at the idea of shutting him up.

'He *hates* it,' Sarah agreed grimly. 'But it works. It keeps him quiet. You only have to threaten to shut him up and he's as quiet as a mouse.'

He hesitated, not liking the idea and uncertain what to say.

'Come on, Arnold, it'll be all right,' Sarah urged.

'Oh, very well,' he agreed in a resigned voice. He was convinced the whole plan would fail and they'd be discovered. They'd *have* to leave then. Perhaps that wouldn't be such a disaster, though. They couldn't go on living here forever . . . or rather they shouldn't, even if they could. He was beginning to see that it wasn't good for the children. They were living in a world of their own, almost completely isolated from the outside world. They grew closer together all the time. It was very cosy, but it wasn't healthy. However, for the moment he'd do his utmost to make this crazy plan for a funkhole work.

He decided on the Plant-Room as the best location for a secret room. Few people ventured there. The din from the air-conditioning plant and the generators during exercises was almost unbearable. Certainly the racket would drown any noise the family made in their hideout. He chose an area masked by one of the huge generators. With the pointed end of a trenching tool he carved a two-foot square on the chalk wall about three feet off the ground and explained his scheme to the children.

'We'll hack a hole into the chalk here. This will be the way in—a hole to crawl through. When we've cut into the chalk for a foot or so we'll start widening out to make a cave inside. It will need to be at least six feet wide and high enough to sit upright in. We'll cover the entrance hole with a sheet of pegboard. That's a kind of hardboard with holes in it. There are sheets of the stuff fixed to the walls for use as noticeboards. We can fix it into position behind us after we're inside.'

'Will we have enough air?' Martin asked anxiously.

'Yes, certainly.'

'Where will we do pee-pees,' Elsie demanded.

'We shall have to use buckets.'

'Ugh!' She made a face.

Darren hadn't grasped any of Mr Godfrey's explanations about the cave but he understood immediately what Elsie was on about.

'If you do hah-hahs in a bucket, it smells,' he declared.

'Yes, well . . .' Mr Godfrey was annoyed at being discomfited by such basic questions and he turned to Sarah and Martin. 'We shall simply have to use plenty of disinfectant. It should only be for two days and nights, thank goodness. And we'll need blankets, torch, water and food—dry food. Chocolate, bread, cheese . . . things like that.'

'I could make sandwiches ready to take,' Sarah suggested. 'It would be like a picnic'.

'We haven't even begun the cave yet,' Mr Godfrey reminded them pessimistically. 'Have you any idea how much solid chalk we have to dig out and remove? Not only remove, but take up into the woods and dispose of. We can't leave it lying around down here.' He made some rough calculations. 'Say six feet by six feet by four feet. That's a hundred and forty-four cubic feet . . . plus the entrance hole—' He stopped, aghast at the result. 'A hundred and fifty cubic feet of chalk!'

They looked at him. The figures conveyed nothing to them.

'How much time do we have?' Sarah asked.

'Two—maybe three—days. We should only count on two.'

'We'd better make a start then,' Martin said, picking up a trenching tool.

Twelve

Saul was by no means clear what he would say to whoever opened the door. He could hardly indulge in outright confrontation: *I'm Sarah's father. Who sent me this note?* Perhaps he should pretend to be his own enquiry agent? *My client has received a very disturbing communication.* Yes, that would be better. No one knew who he was. Saul disliked anything hanging over him and he wanted this business settled. The most likely explanation seemed that Joe Pace had somehow found out about Sarah and wanted to prise money out of Saul.

There was no answer to his ringing. The big old Victorian house had been converted into separate flats, one on each floor. The front door gave access to the hall and stairs and to all the flats except the basement one. Saul contemplated the row of bell-pushes set in the side of the doorframe. Had he been ringing the right bell? The faded card alongside the button read: GROUND FLOOR. No name. Thirteen years was a long time, but he was quite sure it had been the ground floor flat. He could remember the small back room with its single bed and an outlook on to the garden. Carol had been too embarrassed to let him make love to her on the double bed in the front room where she'd slept with her husband.

He was about to ring one of the other bells when he

heard footsteps descending the stairs. The front door opened a few inches and a fat, middle-aged woman peered out at him, breathing heavily.

'Yes? What do you want?'

'I'm looking for the Pace family,' Saul said.

'Pace? Pace? They don't live here no more.'

'Do you know where I could find them?'

She opened the door a little wider and poked her head round like a turtle coming out of its shell. 'What are you—police? Social services?'

'No, I'm from a detective agency,' he lied. 'We're making some enquiries for a client.'

'Oh.' She seemed perplexed. After a pause she said, 'you could try Jean in the basement. She knew 'em well. She might be able to help you.'

'Thanks.' He turned away.

'Mind, she won't be there now—not till the pubs close.'

He nodded and started down the steps to the pavement. Her voice followed him.

'She's much worse, poor cow. Well, who wouldn't be with their little boy lying murdered somewhere.'

He halted, turning round to gape at her.

'You know,' she said impatiently, seeing his blank face, '*Darren*, the little boy who disappeared just before Christmas.'

Mystified, he shook his head.

'Blimey, mate, where you bin. It was in all the papers . . . on the wireless and the telly. Jean's his mother.'

He recalled the case now. He'd been in the States on a business trip and the item had dropped out of the news by the time he returned. Now he came to think of it, Hackney had been mentioned, but he'd seen no report of the actual address. If there had been he would certainly have recognised it as where Carol used to live. Well, that settled it. He wasn't going to impose on a woman whose child had disappeared.

'Yes, I remember,' he mumbled. 'I don't think I'll wait.'

As he started down the steps again there was a sudden squawk from the woman.

'Here's Jean now!'

A youngish woman with brassy hair was approaching, walking with the careful deliberation of the near-drunk. She reached the steps leading to the basement and fumbled with the small wooden gate at the top.

'Jean!' shrieked the woman above him at the front door. 'There's a gent to see you. Wants to know about the Paces.'

Jean's eyes focused on Saul, appraising his well-groomed appearance, the expensive overcoat, the whiff of wealth about him. She hooked a beckoning figure at him.

'C'mon, then,' she invited. 'C'mon down.'

Up above the front door quietly closed. He followed Jean as she clattered on high heels down the steps to the basement door. She had trouble inserting the key. When at last she had the door open she leaned back against Saul, looking up at him over her shoulder. Fumes of gin wafted into his face.

'You're not the law, are you?'

'No.' He changed his story slightly. 'I'm making enquiries for a friend.'

'Thought you weren't the filth,' she said. 'You look too well-heeled for a copper.' She teetered into the flat, waving him in behind her. She peeled off her leather jacket and threw it on to a chair. 'I've had enough of coppers to last me a lifetime. Questions, questions, questions. D'you know—' she wagged a finger in his face, '—the bastards as good as suggested I might have done in my own kid. *Me!*' She sniffed.

'I'm very sorry about your little boy,' Saul said awkwardly. 'I didn't intend to bother you and I was on my way when—'

'It's OK, I'm glad of the company. At the beginning . . .

when it happened, it was all go—visitors every minute of the day. Now, though, no one calls any more.'

She bent and gathered up magazines and clothing from an armchair and deposited them on a sofa. 'Have a seat.' Clearing the other armchair, which was also littered, she sat down opposite him. Her tight black dress rode high above her knees but she made no attempt to pull it down.

'No, no one comes to see me now,' she went on. 'And Bill's left me . . .' Her voice tailed off. She gave a jerky laugh. 'The police thought at first that *Bill*—he's Darren's stepdad—had beaten him so bad he'd killed him and hidden the body. I ask you! Just because he whopped him sometimes. Well, I mean you've to master a boy . . . teach him to behave . . . haven't you? And he was a handful, was Darren, I can tell you! I was going to have him fostered for a while, he was so bad. Give me a rest, like.'

Saul shifted uncomfortably in his chair. He didn't want to listen to this woman's problems. She didn't sound very distressed over her child's disappearance, only annoyed about the accusations. Didn't she wonder what had happened to the boy?

' 'Course I knew Bill hadn't done for him,' Jean went on. 'He wasn't within a hundred miles when Darren went missing. No, I reckon some man took him . . . a queer . . . did things to him . . . then buried him somewhere. Don't suppose we'll ever know.'

Again the absence of emotion. Perhaps she was still in shock, Saul thought? Or maybe she'd done all her crying when it happened, and there was no feeling left in her.

Jean stood up and went to the sideboard. Amid the mess and clutter were some bottles.

'Drink? Whisky?' she bent towards him. Her lipstick had been carelessly applied, giving her mouth a lop-sided look.

'No, no thank you.'

'Coffee, then—you'll have a cup of coffee,' she urged,

'then you can ask me what you want to know.'

He gave in. 'Thank you, yes.'

She went into the kitchen and, through the door, he saw her pick two dirty cups from the sink and rinse them briefly under the tap. His fears were confirmed when a few moments later she handed him a cup of coffee. The rim was encrusted with lipstick and old coffee stains. He transferred the cup to his other hand, turning it round so that he could drink from the other side which was cleaner.

Jean plumped into the armchair again, revealing white briefs between pale parted thighs. She wore neither tights nor stockings. Her legs were painfully thin like the rest of her and the display gave him no pleasure.

'Well?' She gazed at him over the top of the cup, holding it with both hands. 'Who wants to know what—and why?'

'Can we keep names and reasons out of this for the moment?'

'You said you were making enquiries for a friend. OK, so you can leave him out of it, but I want to know who *you* are. I don't talk to people who won't give a name.'

Saul took out one of the firm's business cards. He wasn't going to give her a personal card with his private address and telephone number on it. He wrote his name on the back of the card and handed it to her.

She read his name and giggled. 'Saul? Straight from the Bible, eh? Well, *Saul*,' she said saucily, 'what are you after? If you're a fancy debt-collector looking for Joe Pace, or you're chasing his kids to put them in a Home, you'll get no help from me.'

'No, it's nothing like that,' he assured her. Then he added, cunningly, 'Rather the opposite, in fact. I might be paying *out* some money.' It was half true because he'd probably end up paying somebody to keep their mouth shut. 'Where would I find Mr Pace and family?'

She smiled crookedly. 'Joe Pace is in Maidstone prison, the silly sod. He was done for housebreaking and 'cos he had a couple of pre-cons and a suspended against him, they put him away for eighteen months this time. That was last summer.'

'Is there a Mrs Pace?' He had to ask. It would have been natural for Joe to marry again.

Her smile became twisted. 'No, Joe ain't married. He was once, but his wife died a long time ago. I was just a teenager then but him and me became real close.' Her tone was wistful. 'Not now though.'

'And the children? There were three of them I believe.'

'They took off when Joe went inside. It was the day before the Welfare came along to take them into care. They vanished in the night without a word to anyone. Just packed their things and went. Funny kids. Very secretive. Stuck together more'n most kids. The two girls used to fuss over my Darren, especially Sarah, the older one. She was always washing him and changing his clothes. I let her get on with it. Bit of a madam, she was. Hoity-toity. Know what I mean? She was different from the other girl. A good-looker too.'

It gave Saul an odd feeling listening to her describing Sarah. The girl was his daughter but he knew practically nothing about her. He wondered if Jean knew that she was not Pace's child. If so, *she* could have been the one who sent him that note at Christmas. It didn't seem very likely though. She was more the sort who would ask for money straight away.

'I suppose they were all Mr Pace's children?' he asked casually. 'None of them were adopted or anything?'

'No, 'course not!' Her surprise was genuine, he was sure. 'Oh, they didn't *look* much alike, but they *were* alike . . . underneath. They all came out of the same pod all right.' She laughed crudely. 'And it sure was Joe that seeded the pod!'

113

Unless she was a remarkable actress, it was not Jean who had sent the note. Saul swallowed the rest of his coffee and stood up. There was nothing more to be learned here.

'Thank you for your help. I think I'll try and visit Mr Pace in prison.'

'Yeh, and tell him Jean sends her love.' She gave him a wink and laughed again.

At the door she stood close to him, her small, pointed breasts brushing his coat.

'Wasn't what I told you worth something?'

Saul took a ten pound note from his wallet. She clutched it eagerly. 'Great! I was skint!' Her breast pushed against his arm. 'You get so desperate you'll do anything for money.' She gave him a sexy look. 'Know what I mean?'

Saul stared at her. He could hardly not know what she meant, the way she was rubbing herself against him. She could have been pretty, but her complexion was bad and she'd neglected her teeth. Yet the sudden shock of her blatant invitation brought a surge of desire in him. The sluttish untidiness of the flat had offended him but now, perversely, it excited him. It was this and the fact that she wanted sex with him that caused his arousal. That had always been the trouble with his wife, Louise. She never made advances to him. Never made him feel she wanted him.

'I badly need another tenner.' Jean's voice was a husky whisper.

Perhaps if she hadn't mentioned money again at that point, or the stale smell of the flat hadn't just then risen in his nostrils, he might have taken up her offer. As it was his desire died as quickly as it had risen.

'Yes, well, I'll always be ready to pay for further information.' He opened the door and stepped out.

It was nearing the time for Butch Fearon's discharge from Reading hospital. His dark, curly hair had grown almost to a normal length and he looked very different from the Skinhead who had been rushed into Casualty on an ambulance stretcher some weeks before. Since that time they had mended his body as best they could with surgery and skin grafts; and they had tried to heal his mind with psychotherapy. But the fact was that Butch Fearon's mind and the parts of his body that mattered to him most, were beyond repair and he was obsessed with one thought: *Revenge*. Revenge against the girl who had done this to him. Planning and dreaming was all the comfort Butch had and were the only activities that brought any relief from the mental anguish of being deprived of his precious manhood.

At West End Central police station in London, the photographs of Old Charlie, the man Butch Fearon had kicked to death on the London Underground, were still on display on the public noticeboard, together with the notice appealing for information about his murder.

Thirteen

At the end of the first day's excavation work at Warren Row Mr Godfrey was in despair. He, Martin and Sarah had worked in shifts because only one person at a time could hack away at the two-foot-square hole they were making into the chalk. They had slaved at the task all day and when he went to bed that night he was certain in his own mind that the plan was impractical. Tomorrow he would try to persuade the children to give up the idea and to leave the bunker.

Restless and unable to sleep, he worried over the problem and thought about the coming Civil Defence exercise. The children didn't understand, but *he* knew what it would be like. A pack of men and women in navy-blue battledress and romper suits would be charging around the underground headquarters, enthusiastically pretending to carry out the functions they would supposedly carry out after a nuclear attack. The mock exercises he'd taken part in himself in the past had made him sceptical of the civil defence plans. Did anyone seriously believe that if the unimaginable happened and London were devastated by nuclear missiles these men and women would desert their families? Leave them exposed to all the dangers above ground and slink away to the safety of the bunker? It was unthinkable. And did the planners really think that after a nuclear holocaust the homeless and the sick and injured would take the slightest notice of orders issuing from this underground bunker? The more he dwelt on the dreadful prospect, the less he felt like sleep.

For the first time in many a night he thought of Mrs Godfrey and wondered what she was doing. What had she thought when she learned about the shoplifting charge? Had the police told her of it when she reported him missing or were missing persons dealt with by another part of their organisation? He was ignorant of these matters. Mr Godfrey was happy in his new life, despite its problems, and he had no intention of returning to Mrs Godfrey. She belonged to another existence which was over. He felt a twinge of guilt. Yet maybe she was glad to be rid of him. She'd always seemed to be complaining about him in one way or another. He remembered some of the things she used to say and his guilt dissolved.

In the middle of the night he gave up trying to sleep and went to the kitchen to make a cup of tea. As he waited for the electric kettle to boil he became aware of distant thumping sounds. He moved swiftly towards the Plant-Room which seemed to be the source of the noise.

All four children were there, covered from head to foot in white dust and looking like the little men in a television advertisement for flour. Beyond the small, square entrance hole into the chalk Martin and Sarah had now enlarged the excavation and were able to work back-to-back, half-stooping, half-standing, as they hollowed out the chalk to form a cave. Their eyes and mouths showed as dark slits in the thick white dust covering their faces.

As they shovelled out the broken-up chalk, Elsie and Darren were picking it up and putting it into buckets. Elsie picked up a full bucket.

'Where are you going with that?' Mr Godfrey demanded as she tottered off.

She halted. 'Up top into the woods. I'm spreading the chalk under the bushes to hide it, like you said.'

Suddenly he was ashamed. While he'd been lying in bed fretting and worrying, the children had been slogging away down here. He crawled in beside Sarah and Martin. Both of them were drooping with exhaustion. Gently he pulled the tools from their grasp. It hurt him to see that Sarah's hands were cut and bruised.

'It's the middle of the night and you must get some rest,' he said. 'You've made tremendous progress.' He surveyed their work. The plan *was* possible. 'We'll finish in time now,' he told them. 'Now clean up and off to bed—all of you. I'll carry on.'

By Thursday morning of that week they were putting the finishing touches to the hideout. The work had speeded up as soon as Sarah, Martin and Mr Godfrey were all able to operate at the same time, standing up. They hacked out a recess in one wall of the cave and stacked it with tins of food, biscuits and bottles of water. Blankets and sections of mattresses were brought from the bedding-store and Mr Godfrey helped himself to another, smarter, civil defence uniform from the clothing-store. It would come in handy if for some reason he had to move about the bunker during the exercise.

Sarah and Martin emptied out a small, steel cupboard in the foodstore and carried it into the hideout, laying it horizontally on the floor.

'Whassat for?' Darren asked.

'To shut you up in if you don't behave yourself!' Sarah told him sharply.

Darren lowered his head and cringed and, for once, Mr Godfrey felt sorry for him.

'Where's Darren going to sleep?' Elsie asked, noticing that there was one bedspace too few. 'Is he sleeping with Arnold?'

'No, he is *not* sleeping with me,' Mr Godfrey said tersely.

'I know what, then,' she prattled on, '*I'll* sleep with Arnold and Darren can have my bed.'

'You're a big girl now, Elsie,' said Sarah. 'You can't sleep with Arnold.'

'Why not?' Elsie wanted to know, rolling her eyes.

'Anyway,' Sarah went on, ignoring the question, 'Darren will sleep with me so I can keep an eye on him.'

Mr Godfrey thought the civil defence personnel might start arriving Friday evening or Saturday morning. Certainly they would do so if the exercise was to be this week-end. If not, there would be a week's respite until the following week-end because there were no full-time civil defence staff these days, only part-time volunteers, and exercises had to take place at week-ends when the volunteers were not at their normal jobs. He decided to take no chances.

'We must practise getting into the hideout in a hurry,' he said. 'We should aim to do it within the time it takes someone to come in through the entrance doors and walk down the tunnel to the Plant-Room.'

He made it into a game. 'We'll pretend to be doing our usual things and then I'll give the alarm and we'll see how long it takes us to tidy up and take up position in the hideout.'

'Shouldn't we have a code word for this?' asked Martin. 'Everyone uses code words. You could shout it out and that would be the signal for the alarm.'

'Very well,' Mr Godfrey agreed tolerantly. 'What about "Scramble"?'

'That's old-fashioned, they used it in the last war!' Martin said scornfully.

'"Mothers and fathers",' suggested Elsie, who'd been listening and hadn't understood but was keen to join in.

'"*Pow-Pow*",' shrieked Darren, who not only didn't understand any of it but was engaged in a game of his own making stabbing movements with his fingers as he gunned down imaginary enemies.

'That's it!' declared Mr Godfrey. '"Pow-Pow"! It's perfect.'

They practised *Pow-Pow!* again and again while Mr Godfrey, watch in hand, fussed over the time they took. They tried doing it in the middle of a meal . . . then while they were washing-up . . . watching telly . . . when they were in bed. Mr Godfrey persevered until they could evacuate the bunker every time, leaving no trace of themselves, in four minutes flat. Every time that is except when they pretended to be asleep in bed. Because they were in the dark—and that was how they practised—it never took less than seven minutes from the instant of the alarm to the moment when they were pulling the peg-board into place behind them in the hideout; and Mr Godfrey reckoned this was too long. However, he didn't think the civil defence staff would come in the night.

But, as it happened, they did.

Saul Harrison had decided against going to see Joe Pace in prison. Nothing more had happened since he'd received that upsetting note about Sarah and he was beginning to think he'd allowed himself to read too much into it. For some reason someone had wanted to spoil his Christmas. That was all. The note was not the prelude to a blackmail campaign as he'd feared, otherwise he would have been sent a demand by now. Of course, if the sender was just a mischief-maker there was still the risk that he, or she, would tell his wife, Louise.

That thought sent cold shivers down Saul's spine. Louise could be vicious when she was angry. He could imagine that icy voice of hers. *You mean to tell me you've had a bastard daughter all this time? You've deceived me for thirteen years?* She'd cut him to pieces. *I'll see what Daddy says.* Oh, yes, that was bound to come in to it. Louise was Daddy's darling and although he was old and doddery now, he was as powerful as ever in the business world and Saul still feared him.

Suppose he denied it? There was no *proof* surely? Sarah was registered as Joe Pace's child when she was born, of that he was sure. Who could prove she was really Saul's child? Well, whoever had sent that note knew something. But *proof*? Who would believe without proof? He sighed. Louise would. And she'd tell their daughter Dena. That would hurt him deeply and Louise knew it. She'd always been jealous of the closeness between him and Dena. She wouldn't hesitate to destroy it if she could.

'Pow-Pow!' Mr Godfrey awoke with a start, thinking he'd been dreaming. As he groped for his spectacles he peered short-sightedly at the luminous dial of his watch. The time was two o'clock in the morning.

'Pow-Pow!' It was Darren's voice in the darkness.

'I'll murder the little beast, I swear I will!' Mr Godfrey muttered, struggling up.

Then he heard the alarm buzzer sounding. Suddenly the whole place flooded with light as the overhead striplights came on. He realised that the alarm was genuine. He sprang out of bed and followed the drill they'd practised many times. He reached up and disconnected the electric buzzer behind the light fitting. Hurriedly he tidied the bed, pulled on trousers and jumper, grabbed the rest of his things and went into the corridor. One advantage of abandoning the bunker during the night was that everywhere had been purposely left clear and tidy when they went to bed. The kitchen was bare and spotless and showed no signs of their occupation.

Like well-drilled soldiers, Elsie and Martin ran into the corridor with their clothes under their arms and fell in behind Mr Godfrey waiting to move off in the way they'd rehearsed. An agitated Sarah appeared, Girl Guide tunic over her pyjamas, clutching a bundle of clothing.

'I can't find Darren!' Mr Godfrey's heart missed a beat. 'I've got his clothes *and* his pyjamas, so I don't know what he's wearing. Oh, where can he be?' she wailed.

'Martin . . . you and Elsie go on,' Mr Godfrey urged. 'I'll help Sarah find Darren.'

At the entrance to the headquarters two men in civil defence uniform pulled the massive steel doors wide open. A jeep, with a woman civil defence worker at the wheel, drove inside and the men dragged the doors closed again. The Advance Party for Exercise 'Fallex' had arrived.

Exercise 'Fallex' was the brainchild of a Junior Minister in the Home Office who was trying to convince his sceptical colleagues that the civil defence plans would work even in conditions of severe radio-active fallout after a nuclear attack. He'd appointed one of his under secretaries as the Controller for the exercise. The Under Secretary was young, ambitious and hungry for power. The thought that he would be a kind of dictator in wartime—though he was only playing the part in this exercise—was very much to his liking. One of his first decisions—unpopular with all concerned—was to start the exercise in the middle of the night. He'd sent the Advance Party racing out to Warren Row in the small hours to activate the Headquarters in readiness for the arrival of the Main Party an hour or two later.

The leader of the Advance Party walked briskly down the tunnel, heading for the Plant-Room. His task was to power up the generator and start the air-conditioning plant while the other man went to the communications room and set up the radio links.

Approaching the bottom end of the tunnel he stopped and blinked his eyes in disbelief. A small, nude figure had jumped out from one of the side rooms, poked out a tongue at him—farther than he'd ever seen a tongue put out before—and then scurried away down the tunnel.

'Hey! Hey *you!*'

The man's companion came running up from behind. 'What's the matter? What are you shouting for?'

As the first man turned round to explain, an arm came from another of the side rooms and hooked Darren from sight.

'There's a kid down here.' The leader turned back and pointed. The tunnel, its chalk roof and walls reflecting a brilliant white from the striplights, was deserted.

'Don't be daft! How can there be? The place was shut and barred and there's no other way in.'

'I tell you there was a little boy. He was naked.'

'Naked, eh?' The other man looked sideways at him. 'That fast drive has upset you, old son. You're seeing things.'

'I'm telling you there's a small boy running around down here,' the leader said obstinately.

'OK, let's go back and collect the woman-driver and carry out a search.' He chuckled. 'We'll need her if there's a bare-arsed kid to take care of!'

Behind the hardboard partition wall of the room lower down, Sarah took her hand from Darren's mouth. Mr Godfrey stooped and lifted him up.

'I love you,' Darren cooed, wrapping himself round Mr Godfrey in a bear-like hug.

Sometime later the civil defence trio reached the Plant-Room at the end of their search of the bunker. From behind the sheet of pegboard on the wall by one of the generators, five pairs of eyes watched silently.

Sarah clapped her hand over Darren's mouth again. 'You make just one sound,' she hissed in his ear, 'and I'll shut you up in the box! For *ever!*'

The three civil defence staff hesitated at the door out of the end of the Plant-Room.

'Where does that lead to?' asked the woman.

'Nowhere, as far as I know. But I've never been through there,' replied one of the men.

The two men pushed open the door and went through the short passage to the escape shaft. The team leader waited at the bottom while the other man climbed the rungs to the top of the shaft. After a few moments he came down again.

'It's an airshaft of some kind and its secured on the inside,' he grunted. 'That proves there's no one down here. You saw the size of those doors at the entrance. No kid could open them, even supposing he had a key. It took both of us to pull them open. There's no one but us down here.' He leered at the leader. 'Naked little boy indeed! You've been having naughty thoughts!'

Fourteen

The Main Party poured into the bunker two hours behind the Advance Party. Despite the early hour, and the darkness, they chattered and laughed in the coaches like football supporters. Only the handful of specialists who arrived in their own cars, like the police commander and the army major, were quietly serious.

The Controller arrived last, deliberately. He could perfectly well have been first if he'd wished, but he chose to wait until everyone was inside the bunker before imposing his second unpopular decision on the luckless staff.

'You know who I am?' he snapped at the security guard in the entrance.

The guard wouldn't have known him from Adam if he hadn't been forewarned. He took in the wide gold band on the epaulet of the civil defence battledress and answered promptly:

'Yessir, you're the Controller.'

'Right! Now . . . you've just received a message by despatch-rider from the Home Office War-Room.'

'I have, sir?'

'Yes. It tells you that heavy radioactive fallout is approaching this area and that all air intakes must be closed at once.'

'But, sir, that means shutting off the air-conditioning!'

'That's right. Pass the message to the Operations Room and tell them to do it!'

His eyes gleaming brightly, the Controller strode down the tunnel. He'd show this lot how to run an exercise. He'd make it as near the real thing as you could get.

In the small cave where Mr Godfrey and the children were hiding the effect some hours later, when the air in the Plant-Room had stopped circulating, was every bit as uncomfortable as in the rest of the Headquarters. It grew hot and stuffy and Darren became restless. He was in pyjamas again but quite unable to sleep or to remain in the bed Sarah had made.

'Can't you calm him down?' asked Mr Godfrey, weary of Darren clambering about and trampling on everyone.

Sarah rummaged among the items she had brought into the hideout. Triumphantly she produced a baby's bottle.

'It was Darren's. I brought it away when we collected him.' She gave the bottle a shake and the contents jumped up and down. 'I made him up a mix last night, just in case we needed it. Drinkies?' She held the bottle up. 'Darren loves a bottle, don't you Darren?'

He shook his head violently.

'You always used to,' she said, 'even when you stopped being a baby.' Again he shook his head.

Sarah took a jar of honey from among the tins of food, opened it and dipped the teat in the honey.

'Come along, there's a good boy,' she coaxed, thrusting the bottle at him. He clamped his teeth together, barring entry. Sarah rubbed the teat across his closed mouth. He licked his lips, tasting the honey. She slipped the teat inside and Darren began sucking it greedily.

'There, I said you'd like it.'

Mr Godfrey watched in morbid fascination as Sarah

cuddled the boy to her, crooning softly. A while later Darren's eyelids drooped, his head lolled and the teat slipped from his mouth.

'What's in the bottle?' Mr Godfrey asked, eyeing the dark red mixture suspiciously. Less than a quarter of it had been consumed.

Sarah shrugged. 'This and that.'

'Which and what?' he demanded.

'Oh, it's the sort of stuff his mum used to give him when he was a nuisance. Cough mixture . . . honey—'

'*Cough* mixture? Where did you get cough mixture?'

'I found some in the First-Aid Room.' She showed him the bottle. SLEEPWELL. He'd never heard of it. He scrutinised the label. There seemed to be a remarkably high chloroform and alcohol content.

'This isn't for children, it's for adults only,' he said. 'What else have you put in?'

'Lots of blackcurrant juice to make it taste nice . . . some of the wine left over from Christmas . . . and a handful of aspirins.'

He gazed at the limp Darren, lying unnaturally still.

'You've killed him!'

'Don't be silly!' she laughed. 'His mum used to add an eggcupful of gin. That's *much* stronger. Anyway, I gave him half a cup of this the other night and he slept like an angel. He was quite all right in the morning.'

She laid Darren gently down on a blanket. 'There,' she said, 'now we can all stop worrying and have some peace.'

The protest march from Aldermaston to Trafalgar Square had not had such a good turnout in years. However, some seasoned CND campaigners looked askance at the new faces and provocative banners and placards. This year the Nukes had joined the march and they seemed more concerned about nuclear power stations and the environment than about civil defence and nuclear disarmament. But their numbers were impressive and the aims and interests of the two groups were sufficiently similar for them to make common cause against the government.

The organisers of the march had discovered a new leader. He was a tall, commanding figure of a man. A man of the church, in black clerical hat and cassock. Not a bishop, not a canon . . . simply a priest. But a priest with fire in his belly and an ability to lead people. Father Black got his own way in most things by a mixture of charm and stubbornness. His charm was considerable and this gained him most of the ends he set his mind to; but if charm didn't work he could be very, very obstinate.

The priest had not led the first stage of the march, a token walk from Aldermaston Research Establishment to Reading. That was left to a handful of dedicated CND members who enjoyed re-living the glorious marches of years ago. Father Black had been reserved for the enormous crowd assembled outside Reading railway station.

There were men and women, old and young, and children of all ages, many of them in prams and push-chairs. The crowd had been gathering since midnight and now, while it was not yet dawn on this cold Sunday morning, they were ready to move off. Father Black mounted the flood-lit rostrum that had been erected for him and his words rang out across the heads of the multitude as he bestowed his blessing upon the marchers.

Long before the priest began speaking, messages had been flashing back and forth between the Thames Valley police and the Met. A march of this size needed more of an escort than the usual two constables who had been detailed. By the time Father Black ended his address a police car and several more foot policemen were in attendance and the Met were beginning to worry about the arrangements at Trafalgar Square.

A journalist from the local press had already been

turned out of bed by a telephone call from his editor who had been alerted by a reader whose house overlooked Reading station. Before long the local journalist was to be joined by a pressman from one of the national newspapers and, later in the morning, by a television news cameraman.

Father Black descended from the platform and took his place at the head of the column. With an imperious wave of his hand he gave the signal to move. The march began. He felt in the pocket of his cassock, checking that a piece of paper with instructions on it was still there. He wouldn't need to consult it yet.

In the underground bunker at Warren Row Exercise 'Fallex' was entering its second phase. It was now H+3 in the parlance of civil defence—three days after the nuclear attack. The latest exercise problems were the thousands of homeless roaming the countryside and the gangs of looters pillaging empty houses and terrorising the surviving population.

On the six-foot glass screen in the Operations Room the scientists had plotted the Ground Zeros, calculated the size of the bombs, drawn the wind vectors and predicted the fallout zones. They had overlaid the population maps with the casualty rings and forecast the number of injured and the number of dead. They spoke of megatons and megadeaths instead of millions of tons and millions of deaths. It made the numbers easier to handle on their calculators.

There was a general air of listlessness caused by the stale air in the bunker and everyone was hoping the air-conditioning would be put back on soon.

'Have there been any ill-effects so far, doctor?' the Controller asked the man from the Regional Hospital Board who was the medical adviser.

'No, but I wouldn't advise carrying this experiment any

further. People will become disorientated and they could start to suffer from hallucinations.'

'It won't be for much longer,' the Controller promised. 'I'm calling a conference on the homeless and the looting. I'll announce the all-clear on fallout then and they can open up the entrance doors and re-start the air-conditioning.'

The marchers were well strung out along the road when the procession neared the village of Knowl Hill on the A4. Father Black saw the village sign beside the road and threw out both arms, bringing the leading ranks to a halt. The sergeant in charge of the police escort came walking along the column to join him.

'I'm just letting the stragglers catch up, sergeant,' the priest assured him smoothly.

'Very sensible, Father. Some of the children aren't keeping up too well.'

The priest nodded and as the policeman moved away again he took the slip of paper from his cassock pocket. *At Knowl Hill take the turning to the left off the A4 signposted Warren Row and Catchpole Green. . . .* He shaded his eyes from the early morning sun. Yes, he could see the turning.

He waited patiently for the marchers to compress into a solid column once more. When he was satisfied that he had a packed mass at his back he raised his arm and flung it forward in the signal to move. As he reached the turning Father Black signalled with his arm as though he was driving a car and the leading ranks, five or six abreast, obediently turned left along the road to Warren Row.

The police sergeant had dropped back to the middle of the procession and was chatting to the policewoman who'd been included in the escort party in case of problems with the women and children. He'd grumbled at first when they'd suddenly cancelled his rest day and told him to handle this caper. But he was on overtime and it was a sight better than being detailed for the Met reinforcements at Wembley next week which he'd now be excused from. Soon he'd be handing over the march to the Met when it reached the county boundary and then he could nip smartly home. It was early in the year but there was a promise that today would turn out to be one of those warm, near-Spring days and he'd be able to do some work in the garden.

Suddenly he realised that the head of the column was no longer proceeding along the A4 but had disappeared up a turning to the left and the whole procession was following.

'Where the Hell are they going?'

He set off at a trot. When he caught up with the constable at the head who was arguing with the priest, there was a hundred yards of the column already wending its way along the country lane.

'What's going on?' the sergeant panted, falling into step.

'He refuses to stop!' said the outraged constable.

'We've taken a small detour through the countryside, that's all,' said the priest soothingly. 'It's a lovely morning and that main road is very boring.'

'You shouldn't have done that without asking, sir,' the sergeant told him sharply. For a moment he contemplated turning the column round and then quickly abandoned the idea. In this narrow road there would be chaos. Better to let them go on. 'Very well, but you must follow my directions from now on.' He turned to the constable. 'Nip back to the patrol car at the rear. Tell them to let Force HQ know there's been a change of plan. We'll be rejoining the A4 at Littlewick Green.'

The sergeant fell in behind Father Black and alongside the leading file. No particular route had been laid down

131

for the march towards London, so long as it crossed the Thames at Maidenhead. There hadn't been much time to consider routes because until last night no one had expected more than the usual handful of marchers and everyone had assumed they would follow the A4 to the Met boundary. It didn't matter much and he'd soon have them on the main road again. All the same the sergeant felt uneasy.

Darren woke on that Sunday morning while the others still slumbered. He was well refreshed after his long, half-drugged sleep but everyone else was exhausted from lack of sleep the previous night when the Advance Party had arrived. Darren badly needed to pee but he didn't want to use the smelly bucket in the corner. Besides the noise might wake the others and they'd shut him up or make him go to sleep again.

He considered just lying there and wetting; but he was in Sarah's bed and she might wake up if he made it wet. He decided to use the big loo that he was used to. Carefully he edged away from the sleeping Sarah and put on his shoes. Crawling to the exit he squinted through the holes in the pegboard covering. There was no one out there. Sarah had told him that if the people out there caught him they'd take him away and shut him up and then take him back to his stepfather; but Sarah sometimes told fibs. Besides, they'd have to catch him first.

He pushed the pegboard away, clambered out and hung it in place again. He toddled off through the Plant-Room, out into the tunnel and headed for the lavatories.

Fifteen

The two civil defence men of Reconnaissance Unit No. 3 sat in their R/T jeep at the side of the road by Lot Wood enjoying the sunshine. They knew, from the earlier chit-chat over the radio, what conditions were like in the bunker and they were thankful that they were up here in the fresh air. Their part in the exercise was to take readings of the radioactivity in the area with their geiger counters and radiation meters and to radio the information to the communications room in the underground headquarters.

The man operating the transmitter was amazed to see a column of marchers appear round a bend in the road and trek towards them.

'Cripes! They've actually mustered some volunteers to act as Homeless. Hundreds of them!'

'Are you sure they're part of our exercise?' asked his companion.

'Yes, of course. Look at all those women and kids . . . and the prams. Someone's trying to catch us napping. We must notify Headquarters at once.' He flicked the switch on the microphone.

'Hallo, X-ray 6! Hallo, X-ray 6! this is Romeo 3, Romeo 3.'

'Go ahead Romeo 3.'

'Many Homeless heading along Warren Row Road . . .'

The other man stood up in the open vehicle and stared over the top of the windscreen. 'Hang on a moment, I think they're carrying placards.' The wireless operator, engrossed in his R/T procedures, carried on sending.

'It's the Aldermaston March!'

The wireless operator finished the message and signed off. 'Can't be,' he declared, 'not on this road. And anyway, there are far too many of them. The march was down to half a dozen Buddhist monks last year.'

'Use your eyes man! You can *read* the placards now.'

The operator looked. There was no need to strain his eyes.

NUCLEAR POWER—IT'LL COST THE EARTH   NO TO NUCLEAR HOLOCAUST REMEMBER HIROSHIMA   REMEMBER NAGASAKI SHELTERS FOR ALL

Dolefully, he picked up the microphone again. He was a good operator and he followed the correct procedure exactly—and that was what caused all the trouble. If he'd simply *cancelled* the previous message all would have been well. But in situations like this, when events in the 'real' world impinged on an exercise, there was a strict rule: messages about 'real' events had to be prefixed with the words NOT-EX meaning *NOT AN EXERCISE MESSAGE BUT A REAL ONE.*

Dutifully, the operator began his transmission:

'NOT-EX . . . I say again NOT-EX.' Then followed the message:

'Aldermaston marchers proceeding in strength along Warren Row Road towards Lot Wood. Now at map reference 821805.'

In the communications room of the underground head-quarters the Traffic Supervisor also followed strict procedure. Since this was information about a real demon-stration march he routed the message he had written down to the police commander. Trouble was, the first message was already in the hands of the controller.

Further along the bunker, in the gent's lavatory, a sleepy-eyed man just off shift-duty opened his trousers and squared up to the wall-mounted urinal bowl. Suddenly he became aware of a small boy in pyjamas three stalls to his right.

'Hullo, son,' he said automatically, not immediately registering anything amiss.

Darren beamed at him. 'I love you,' he said.

With a start the man was fully awake and so astonished that he missed his target. Unable to stop, his sphincter muscle powerless against the pressure of a full bladder, he splattered the wall. Hurriedly he corrected his aim. When he looked round, the boy had vanished. The man shook his head vigorously.

'Must be lack of oxygen,' he muttered. 'I'd better tell the doc.'

The Controller's conference began badly. The air in the room was foul and the humidity was stifling. One human being gives off about a gallon of water vapour every twenty-four hours in the form of sweat, and moisture in the breath. Normally this moisture evaporates into the surrounding air. Put sixty or seventy people down a bunker and cut off the air circulation however, and you have an awful lot of water vapour with nowhere to go. The air becomes too saturated to retain any more moisture and every surface runs wet with condensation.

The Controller had come to the exercise suitably pre-pared and had changed into a short-sleeved sweat-shirt and lightweight cotton trousers. The Medical Officer had stripped to his vest and pants. This was partly for comfort, partly because he wanted to make the Controller feel silly but mainly because he didn't give a damn for anyone. The police commander, who was thankful that he'd decided against wearing uniform for the exercise, had removed his jacket, loosened his tie and rolled back his shirt cuffs. He looked like an American film detective. The army major remained in full uniform. Purple faced . . . impeccable.

The Medical Officer cleared his throat. 'I think you should restore the air circulation, Controller.'

'When I've studied the scientific officer's report on the radio-active fallout,' said the Controller tersely.

You jumped-up little Hitler, keeping people in conditions like this just to show off your authority, thought the M.O. Aloud, he said:

'I've already had one report of a man hallucinating.'

'Really?' The police commander showed interest. 'What sort of hallucination was it?'

'He imagined he saw a small boy in pyjamas in the gent's lavatory.'

'Oh, *that* sort,' murmured the army major.

'Pay attention, please,' the Controller rasped. 'We have to decide what to do about the looting. Also, I've just received another message about homeless. Apparently they're milling about on the roads near here. We must—'

'Mr Controller,' interrupted the M.O. in an ominous tone, 'are you, or are you not, accepting my advice to restore the air-conditioning?'

'All *right!*' the Controller snapped. He turned to the clerk at his elbow. 'Tell Operations that we're clear of fallout and they can unseal the air vents and start up the air-conditioning.'

'Ask them to open the entrance doors as well to clear the air quickly,' added the Medical Officer. He caught the Controller's glare. 'Well, there's no reason not to, is there?'

The Controller, unable to think of an objection, nodded to the clerk. 'Now perhaps, we may return to our problem,' he said sourly. 'This looting business . . . I propose to use the ultimate sanction.'

The Medical Officer fixed jaundiced eyes upon him. 'And what the Hell does that mean?'

'The ultimate sanction?' The Controller rolled the words round his tongue. He liked their sound. They were the Minister's words. Like most politicians the Minister avoided the direct word for anything unpleasant. 'It means, gentlemen, that in time of war I have the power of life and death. There's only one way to stop looting.'

They looked at one another.

'You mean . . . top 'em?' asked the army major.

'Yes.'

'Good God!' The major sucked in his cheeks.

The police commander tried hard to project his thoughts into the future and to imagine the situation they were discussing. The solution seemed far-fetched but he supposed he'd better go along with it. The Chief Constable had told him the Home Office attached great value to these exercises and that he was to back the Controller at all times. Doubtfully, he agreed. 'Yes, I suppose it might stop looting if you hanged a few.'

'Firing squad,' said the major promptly.

'I beg your pardon?'

'Mustn't hang 'em, y'know. We'd be under Military Law. You'd shoot 'em. Have to be a Court-Martial, of course. Wouldn't be legal otherwise.'

'These are *civilians*,' the Controller protested. 'If the Civil Power orders the execution—'

'Oh, stuff it, all of you!' cried the Medical Officer who had stood up to study the map on the wall. 'They're all doomed to die in any case.' He pointed to the transparent overlay the scientific officer had pinned to the map. 'The looting was reported *here* in an area of heavy fallout.' He circled it with his finger. 'Everyone in that area will have received a fatal dose of radiation. They'll be dead within three days. There's no sense in hanging *or* shooting them.'

'That's not actually the point, doctor,' said the Controller smugly. 'We have to make an example of them as a warning to others, don't you see?'

The M.O. gaped at him incredulously. Then a huge grin spread over his face. 'And no doubt you'll be having their bodies dangled from trees by the roadside like they did in the old days?'

'This is a very serious business!' the Controller said angrily. 'Here we are, faced with a complete breakdown of law and order . . . possibly anarchy, murder and rape . . . and all you can do is to make jokes! We *must* keep control. Can't you understand that?'

If this happened, the M.O. was thinking, *if this really happened, you'd be a Dictator and you'd love every minute of it.* The thought was too awful to contemplate and he closed his eyes and shook his head. He was glad he was retiring soon. He and his wife planned to emigrate. They would see their time out abroad—in the Caribbean probably—away from this madness.

'We're agreed then?' The Controller glanced round the table. 'We execute looters?' No one spoke. 'Right! I'll send a message to all units.' He stood up. 'Conference is adjourned!' He went out.

The Medical Officer opened his eyes again. 'He's mad, you know. A clear case of paranoia. If we had him in charge in a nuclear war we'd have to lock him up and one of us would have to be the Controller. Frightening thought, isn't it?'

The sound of the air-conditioning plant starting up woke Sarah in the hideout. She patted the vacant space beside her and sat up quickly.

'Darren's gone!'

The other three came awake. Like Sarah they had gone to sleep fully dressed.

'We must find him quickly or we'll all be in trouble,' Mr Godfrey said grimly. Hastily he pulled on the new civil defence battledress he'd brought into the cave with him. With luck he would be able to move around in the bunker without being challenged.

'I'm coming too,' said Sarah, picking up Darren's anorak. 'He might run away from you.'

Mr Godfrey hesitated. In her Girl Guide uniform she *could* pass for a civil defence messenger at a quick glance . . . except for that long blonde hair.

'All right. But put on your beret.'

Darren, on his way back from the lavatory to the Plant-Room, paused in the doorway to a sleeping cubicle. Until last night this was where he and Elsie had slept. A loud snore reverberated the hardboard partitions. It was too much for Darren. He went in.

Most of the lights at this end of the tunnel were out and in the gloom he had to go to the head of the bed before he could see who was in it. It was a young woman—one of the off-duty shift—and she was covered only by a sheet. He stood there, puzzled, his face on a level with hers.

'I love you,' he said tentatively.

The response was another loud snore. Darren moved down the bed. Would she be the same as Elsie, he wondered? He knew what Elsie was like under her nightie but he had an idea that big girls were different. Lifting the sheet with one hand, he delved into the warmth beneath with the other.

Sixteen

Reconnaissance Unit No. 3 had withdrawn nearly a mile along the road to the junction of Pudding Hill and Hodgedale Lane. Once again the Aldermaston march was nearing their position and the civil defence men had received no instructions and didn't know what to do. However, the march appeared peaceful and well-behaved and they were relieved to see a burly police sergeant plodding along beside the leaders.

Father Black, at the head of the column, was disappointed.

We know there's a secret government exercise this week-end, the organisers of the march had told him *and we know the wartime Headquarters is in that area, but we don't know exactly where. There should be a high wireless mast somewhere—all these controls have one. Head for that.*

The priest surveyed the skyline. No mast stood above the pine trees, no sound disturbed the gentle Berkshire countryside on this sunny Sunday morning. Earlier he thought he'd seen a vehicle, in the dark-green of civil defence, on the road ahead of them, but he wasn't sure and it had gone now. He lifted his eyes Heavenwards and appealed to Higher Authority for guidance.

Down below in the bunker the police commander had been handed the second message sent by the Recce Unit—the one prefixed NOT-EX which told him the Aldermaston marchers really *were* moving along Warren Row road. He concluded, wrongly as it happened, that they knew the location of the bunker and were headed for it. He also concluded, this time rightly, that the police escort with them would be unaware of the existence of the secret headquarters because this was known only to the Chief Constable, the Assistant Chief Constable and himself.

He lifted the telephone. 'Get me Police Headquarters! Quickly!' When the connection was made he identified himself to the Thames Valley information room. Then:

'Is there an R/T car with the Aldermaston march?' he asked. 'Good. Patch me through to it.'

The police patrol car was leisurely keeping station with the rear end of the march. Trailing behind in another car were a television news cameraman and a sound recordist. They'd shot a few feet of film along the road and had been about to hare off to Heathrow to catch the arrival of a pop star, when the march had suddenly turned aside from the A4. The news team hung on, hoping for a story, but nothing more happened. They dropped behind and were preparing to turn round when the police car in front of them suddenly came to life.

The two constables had been galvanised into action by a few sharp sentences from the police commander over the radiotelephone link.

'Where are the marchers now?'

'Approaching the junction of Hodgedale Lane and Pudding Hill, sir—that's half-a-mile from the village of Warren Row.'

'They must be stopped! They're practically on top of us!'

'Beg pardon sir, where are you?'

'Damn near under your feet.'

The two constables exchanged looks. The police commander was on secondment from the Met and this was presumably some private joke of his.

'Sir?'

'Never mind. Get to the head of the column and halt it! Tell whoever's in charge of the escort to turn the march back to the A4. *Now*. It must not proceed any further along that road. It should never have been allowed this way in the first place.'

The police car pulled out from the rear of the column, blue light flashing, siren honking, and began forcing its way past the marchers on the narrow road. The television news crew immediately abandoned their turn and chased after it.

In another hundred yards Father Black would have espied the aerial mast on top of Pudding Hill and, if he'd been left alone, he'd have triumphantly led the marchers up there and they would have tramped harmlessly around the base of the mast. It was the radio mast for the underground headquarters all right, but it was a good quarter-of-a-mile away from the hidden entrance in the woods and it gave no clue to the position of the bunker.

The police car drew level with the sergeant at the front of the column. 'Message from Force HQ,' they told him. 'The marchers must not proceed any further along this road. They're to be turned round and escorted back to the main road.'

The sergeant swore. 'Bloody Hell! That's easier said than done.'

The patrol car roared fifty yards ahead and slewed across the road. One of the constables emerged grasping a loud-hailer. Father Black and the leading marchers hesitated, took a few more steps and then halted and waited expectantly. Behind them the crowd closed up, trapping the news team's car. The cameraman and the sound recordist made their way forward on foot as the people fell silent awaiting the policeman's announcement.

Then, into the quiet, from further along the road beyond the police car, the civil defence vehicle's wireless suddenly blared forth the Controller's message to all units.

'Thousands of homeless and undesirables are roaming the countryside, many of them in the vicinity of this headquarters. Looting has taken place. The Regional Controller, in exercise of his emergency powers, has decreeed that anyone found looting shall be summarily executed. All units note and advise local population. Message ends.'

There was a shocked silence. The policeman paused uncertainly with the loud-hailer halfway to his mouth. Then a roar of anger and disapproval rang forth from the marchers and with one accord they surged forward; but the police car drawn across the narrow road and practi-cally touching the bank on either side, effectively blocked their path. The crowd began jumping the ditch at the side of the road and scrambling over the bank and into the woods beyond to avoid the block. As the head of the column broke ranks so the whole march turned sideways and headed into the woods.

The camera team began filming, not at all sure of what was going on, but sensing a drama unfolding. They had been all set up to record whatever the police had to say when they halted the march and had captured every word of that incredible announcement that had seemed to materialise out of the air. There had to be a story here. Hopefully they trundled after the tall, dark figure of Father Black.

Down below, the civil defence staff had started to haul aside the heavy entrance doors . . .

In a sleeping cubicle a young woman turned over in her

sleep, trapping Darren's searching hand between her crossed thighs . . .

The handset in the police car crackled angrily as the commander demanded information.

'They've taken to the woods, sir, the whole blessed lot of them. There was this daft announcement about executing people. It came over the radio of a civil defence vehicle parked along the road here. The crowd went wild when they heard it.'

'Oh, my God!' groaned the commander.

Those on the flank, who had penetrated deepest into the wood, saw some chain-link fencing. Curiously, they changed direction towards it.

The police sergeant caught up with Father Black who had stopped about a hundred yards into the wood and was awaiting a further sign from the Almighty. The sergeant grasped the priest's arm.

'This is far enough, sir,' he said firmly. 'Lead your people back to the road please.'

Deeper in the wood some of the marchers following the chain-link fencing had come to the open gates. Inside, on a slope leading down into the ground, were several dark-green civil defence vehicles.

'Over here Father!' they shouted. 'This way!'

The priest shook his arm free of the policeman's grip. 'Heaven has given a sign!'

The astonished sergeant hesitated. There wasn't another police uniform in sight and, in any case, the priest was committing no offence. Also, he was uncomfortably aware of the cameraman now dogging their every move. He decided not to prevent Father Black moving off towards the distant shouts of 'Over here Father!', but simply to accompany him. He noticed the police car move further along the road and then turn into the wood through an open gate away to his right. There appeared to be a track leading down from the gate to the place where the priest was heading and the crowd was gathering.

In the bunker's sleeping quarters a woman screamed. Darren had at last freed his hand. As he scuttled out along the tunnel like a frightened crab, Sarah spotted him and gave chase. A young woman ran from the cubicle clutching a sheet around her nakedness and grabbed Mr Godfrey as he was about to follow after Sarah. She started babbling at him.

The Controller had returned to the conference room after despatching his message. He listened to the police commander's first words and boggled.

'You mean the Aldermaston marchers are coming *here*? *Now*?'

'Coming through the woods above our heads this very moment. About two thousand of them.'

'What fun,' muttered the Medical Officer. The temperature hadn't dropped yet and he was still in his vest and pants. The Controller, however, had now donned his uniform.

'But they mustn't! I won't allow it!' cried the Controller. 'I'll soon put a stop to this! I'm going up to the entrance.' He hurried out.

'Why don't you try hanging the first two who set foot inside?' the M.O. shouted after him gleefully. He rubbed his hands together between his knees and chuckled loudly. 'Oh, this is going to be great! This I must see!' He rose and followed the Controller.

The army major dusted an imaginary speck of dust from his highly-polished Sam Browne. He gazed after the departing doctor, wrinkling his nose in distaste at the hairy legs and the rumpled underclothes that were grubby from doing duty as outer garments for the last twenty-four hours. He snorted and turned to the police commander.

'Fancy letting demonstrators see him dressed like that! And he thinks the *Controller* is balmy?'

But the police commander was busy on the telephone to Force Headquarters, ordering up police reinforcements.

Sarah had cornered Darren in an empty store-room. She approached him warily, holding out his anorak. If only she could bundle him up she might yet manage to return him to their hideout without anyone noticing.

'Put your coat on,' she urged. 'You can't run around in pyjamas.'

'No! Don't want to!' Darren shouted crossly. 'It's pissing hot!'

'I've brought your titty-bottle,' she said artfully, pulling it out and waving it slowly from side to side. Darren's piggy eyes watched the movement like a patient's eyes following a hypnotist's finger. His last drink had been over twelve hours ago and he was exceedingly thirsty.

Sarah could read him like a book and she correctly interpreted the expressions flitting across his face.

'Have a little drinkies and Sarah will cuddle you,' she coaxed.

Mr Godfrey tried to calm the hysterical woman who was now leaning on his shoulder sobbing. So far no one else had appeared and he was anxious to get away from her before anyone challenged him.

'I expect it was someone's little boy,' he said soothingly. 'They're not supposed to bring children on exercises, of course, but perhaps they couldn't find a baby-sitter—or maybe they were given permission.' This was wildly improbable but it was all he could think of to say in the time.

The woman stifled her sobs and lifted her head from his shoulder.

'He wasn't *human*,' she said. 'He was a— a—' She searched for a word. '—a kind of monster—a small monster. He had slits for eyes and his face was screwed up as though he was permanently grinning. It was *horrible!*'

That's our Darren, thought Mr Godfrey.

'That was no little boy,' the woman went on confidently. 'Why, his *thing* was this long.' She went to hold her hands apart to demonstrate but the sheet began to slip and she thought better of it. 'Sticking up in front, half as long as his body it was.'

Just Darren up to his usual tricks, Mr Godfrey could have told her. She'd surprised Darren and he would do what he always did in a crisis—he'd grab his penis and start pulling it about. Inevitably, it would respond. The erect organ of a small boy was out of all proportion to his body—something most women didn't realise. However, she'd given him an idea.

'Ah,' he said, 'you've had a *nightmare*. It's the lack of air in this place and the heat and the damp.' He watched her swallow the suggestion. 'Now, you go back to bed,' he advised, 'and I'll have someone look in on you.'

The police sergeant made a final attempt to save the situation. Father Black's flock was gathering behind him again and instinct warned the sergeant that there would be trouble if the demonstrators went through those gates, although he had no idea what was in there—it looked to be just a fenced-off section of the wood. The patrol car was making its way along the track towards them and he could see one or two of his constables and the policewoman converging fast. If he could somehow delay the demonstrators for a minute or so . . .

He sprinted ahead to the gates and, standing between

them, extended his arms. They nowhere reached the sides.

Father Black, with a solid phalanx of men, women and children at his back, moved relentlessly towards him. Thirty yards . . . twenty . . .

The driver of the police car bumping along the track at right angles to the column saw the narrowing gap and accelerated, siren wailing, hoping to scatter the marchers and straddle the gates before they reached them.

Father Black, undeterred by the police car bearing down on him, marched on. 'Stand aside, sergeant!' He was less than ten yards away. Swiftly the sergeant assessed the situation. It was too late for the police car to intercept now without mowing down the leading ranks. The determined press of humanity behind the priest would trample him into the ground, the sergeant decided. He moved aside.

The police driver stood on his brakes and the car slithered over the rough ground and shuddered to a halt within inches of a woman pushing a baby in a pram. She jabbed her fingers upwards in a rude sign at the driver and walked on through the gates.

The Controller ran up the tunnel towards the entrance.

'Close the doors!' he screamed at the confused civil defence men standing there. But there was no time. A tall, forbidding figure in priest's cassock was already striding down the slope towards the entrance, followed by a seething mass of people.

The Controller rushed out through the doors, halted and threw up his arms dramatically.

'Stop!' he shouted. 'Stop! You mustn't come down here!'

Father Black's step never faltered. God was on his side.

The Controller moved forward again shouting:

'Back! Back I say!' God was on his side too. A different God. A God who dealt in megadeaths.

The two men came face to face. 'You can't come in here! It's *secret!*' the Controller cried desperately.

The priest paused, very briefly and for a moment his hand rested gently on the Controller's shoulder.

'I understand, my son. I understand.' The gentle hand became a grip of steel and propelled the Controller to one side. 'But it's God's Will.' He marched purposefully on and the Controller was engulfed by the human tide flowing behind him.

As Father Black covered the last few yards to the entrance doors he could see into the downward sloping tunnel. Dark-clothed figures in battledress ran agitatedly back and forth under the bright lights and a blast of hot foetid air welled out into the priest's face.

'Holy Mother of God!' he muttered. ''T'is the stench of evil. And will y'look at that, now. 'T'is like the Gates of Hell itself!'

At the entrance he passed a figure in vest and pants, a man grimacing and laughing. The M.O. had just seen the Controller go down for the third time in a tangle of children and pushchairs. Quickly the priest crossed himself and hurried on. Behind him a multitude flooded into the bunker. The cameraman was borne in on the first wave, filming frantically as he grasped the significance of his surroundings. In three minutes the invaders outnumbered the inhabitants five to one. In ten the bunker was completely overrun.

Sarah had administered only a little of Darren's bottle to him when the uproar erupted. She raised her head and found three or four children gawping curiously in the doorway of the store-room where she sat holding Darren. Darren opened his eyes and saw the children. He spat out the bottle-teat and jerked himself out of Sarah's arms. Enraged he threw himself at the watching children who were laughing and pointing at him. They scattered as he hurled himself after them, mouthing and spitting.

'Darren! Darren, come back!' Sarah ran out into the corridor and stopped, stupefied at the sight of all the people.

The Controller fought his way back to the conference room. 'This is a riot, I'm calling the military,' he gabbled, grabbing a telephone.

'You'll do no such thing!' bawled the army major, clamping his hand over the Controller's and preventing him from lifting the receiver. '*I'm* in command of the local army units. They go to the aid of the civil authority only at the request of the senior police officer on the scene and no one else.' He glanced at the police commander.

'Keep out of this,' the commander told the Controller curtly. 'You've done enough damage. We're not in your bloody exercise now!'

Seventeen

Exercise 'Fallex' collapsed in chaos. It was doomed from the moment Father Black led his followers through the entrance to the underground bunker. It was probably doomed after the Reconnaissance Unit had sent its two messages. Perhaps, even earlier than all that, disaster had been pre-ordained when the Minister appointed a man like the Under Secretary to be the Controller.

Father Black was delighted with his achievement. He'd succeeded beyond all his expectations and without any violence or the breaking of a single law. True, there was the trifling matter of trespass, but nothing would come of that. He sat in the Controller's conference room perched on the table swinging his legs and smiling benevolently as he patted the heads of the children who milled around him. They were watching the television team setting up their equipment in readiness for an interview. A small boy, who seemed to be wearing pyjamas under his anorak, stared up at the priest, his pale blue eyes crinkled in a smile.

'I love you, man in black,' he said.

'I love you too, my child.' Fondly, the priest ruffled the fair curls.

The camerman saw his opportunity for an opening sequence and quickly trained his camera. A Girl Guide, with long golden hair, obstructed his view. Sarah, who'd lost her beret as she chased through the crowd, was dragging Darren bodily away from the priest. Darren had never seen a man dressed like Father Black before and he was trying to raise the skirt of his cassock to look underneath. The cameraman changed to a close-up of Father Black's expression, cutting out Darren but taking several frames of Sarah as he zoomed in.

A video recording of the news film had been brought to the Minister's house for him to see. Father Black had secured the finest propaganda slot he could have wished for—the leading item in the television news. He'd prepared a speech for delivery at Trafalgar Square at the end of the march but he had given parts of it direct to the cameras at Warren Row.

'The Western World,' he intoned, 'spends twenty times as much money on weapons and military forces . . . civil defence . . . and—' He made one of those dramatic pauses he was so good at in the pulpit. '—and the *filth* of war, as it does on aid to the sick and the dying of the Third World. And to what end? *To what end?*' the priest trumpeted. At this point the producer brought in, as an overvoice, the recorded wireless message about executing looters. The overvoice faded again as Father Black ended: '*That* is the kind of world the Government is planning for us!'

The Minister seemed to be grinding his teeth together. He'd be the laughing stock of Whitehall! The Opposition would crucify him. His wife hastily relieved him of the brandy glass he was holding as he howled for the Controller to be brought to him. *Now! This instant!*

The Minister was not a man to admit to any error in his own judgement. Troubles were made by 'wretched civil servants'—in this case by the Under Secretary in his own

Department whom he'd selected as the Controller for the exercise. He lost no time in unleashing his rage upon the man.

'God knows what you were thinking of with that lunatic message! And how could you be so insane as to coop people up like that! The papers are having a field day—not to mention the current affairs programmes on TV. Have you seen the cartoon in the *Mail*? *Shut up damn you!*' he shouted as the Under Secretary went to speak. 'Do you realise the consequences? That place was Top Secret. *Top Secret!* Now we shall have to declassify it.' The Minister made a moaning sound. 'The expense. All that careful planning up the spout. We'll have to abandon the place now—strip it out.' Savagely he snarled at the Under Secretary: 'See if you can manage *that* within the next month without any more cock-ups!'

Peace had returned to the bunker that Sunday surprisingly quickly. Father Black had led his jubilant troops out again scarcely half an hour after they'd entered.

'A sit-in, I think they call it these days,' he'd explained courteously to the police commander. 'It will be quite short. We've made our protest and we shall leave peacefully.'

The policeman had been extremely relieved. The last thing he wanted to do was to order in the posse of police waiting outside the bunker. He could see a very tricky situation would develop in the confines of the bunker. He'd made a brief tour of the headquarters and no one was doing any wrecking, although he'd come across children poking into some of the equipment. The Controller would have had a fit if he'd seen them. However, the commander had confined the Controller to his room until the demonstration was over.

'But people are *playing* with the maps in the Operations

Room! They're moving the pins about and muddling the messages,' the Controller had wailed.

'Think yourself lucky that's *all* they're doing,' he'd retorted. 'I couldn't do much about it even if I wanted to, which I don't. I can't use force with all these women and children about so there's no point in bringing the heavies down here.'

Half an hour later, true to his word, Father Black had led the marchers out. Soon after, the civil defence personnel had begun pulling out. There had been a terse, plain language directive from the Home Office War Room where the day's events had been monitored: NO SPEAK PRESS CLOSE DOWN EVACUATE CONFIRM COMPLETION SOONEST.

There had been some nasty moments for Mr Godfrey and the children as the Rear Party checked round to see that no one had been left behind and that everything was switched off and safe. They were safely back in their hideout and Sarah had fed Darren a massive dose of his knock-out drink.

'How will we know when everyone's gone?' Martin asked in a whisper. The generator had stopped and the Plant-Room was silent.

'They'll switch off the rest of the lights—at least they *should*,' Mr Godfrey said, wondering if the lights had been left on by mistake since there had been no sound nor sign of activity for some time.

'I'm hungry,' Elsie complained. 'And all the chocolate's gone.'

'Shh!' warned Mr Godfrey. The Plant-Room door had opened.

Two men entered. They were the same two men as yesterday morning. Then they had been the Advance Party. Now they were the Rear Party. They walked through and into the passage to the escape shaft. After a while they returned and walked slowly round the room

154

looking under the generators and into possible hiding-places. They had received strict instructions to double-check that not one of the army of demonstrators had been left behind and was hidden away in the bunker.

'They're checking every inch of the place,' breathed Mr Godfrey, who was observing through the holes in the pegboard. Quietly he moved away as the men came near.

At that moment Darren uttered a long shuddering sigh from the depths of his stupor.

'What was that?' one of the men asked.

Sarah flung a blanket over Darren's head and they sat motionless, holding their breath.

'I didn't hear anything,' answered the other man.

'It sounded like someone sighing.'

'*Sighing?*' The man laughed uproariously. 'It must be that naked little boy you thought you saw yesterday. *I'm* sighing. Sighing for a pint! Come on, we've checked the place thoroughly. I reckon we've earned a drink.'

The hospital staff were glad to see the last of Butch Fearon. He'd been a morose and difficult patient and the ward nurses were frightened of him when he looked at them with those cold pitiless eyes.

His Skinhead cronies, Sid and Terry, had visited him only once more after that first time. They'd found it hard to communicate with him and they hadn't visited again.

'I thought a guy didn't get the urge after he'd lost his balls,' Sid said to Terry, 'but it ain't like that. Butch still gets the feeling, poor sod, but he can't do nothing about it . . . can't relieve himself no way. It's sending him round the bend.'

'It's doing that all right,' Terry agreed. 'He talks about nothing else but finding that stupid chick that done this to him and what he's gonna do to her when he catches up with her.' He shivered. 'Poking the bitch is one thing— I'd go along with that, if he ever found her. But the way

Butch tells it he wants to waste the chick. He means it, Sid! Jesus, I ain't into killing! Not me! He'd better not come looking to me to help him!'

But Butch did.

After the bunker had been evacuated and closed up that Sunday evening Mr Godfrey and the children took a cautious look round and re-established themselves in their old quarters. The staff had departed hurriedly and no attempt had been made to clear up. The place was a shambles. Blankets and bedding had been left lying about and there was dirty crockery everywhere.

'Like the wreck of the *Mary Celeste*,' Mr Godfrey murmured as they looked in the kitchen.

'What's the *Mary Celeste*?' asked Martin.

'She was a brigantine found abandoned in the Atlantic. It was in the days of sail, of course. 1872, I think. All her gear was intact and the galley looked as though the crew had just had a meal. Yet there wasn't a soul on board and none of the crew were ever found.'

'How creepy,' said Sarah as she tut-tutted about the kitchen surveying the mess.

Elsie returned from an inspection of the Recreation Room. 'It's OK,' she said, 'the telly still works.' Her wants were simple: telly and food.

That evening they gathered to watch the news to see if the invasion of the bunker would be reported. It was the first item.

'Ooh look, there's Sarah!' cried Elsie. For a few seconds there were shots of an anxious-faced Sarah before Father Black's face occupied the screen in frame-filling close-up.

'What's he looking so worried about?' asked Martin.

'Darren was getting under his skirt-thing,' said Sarah.

'I love that man in black,' Darren announced. He jumped off Sarah's lap. 'He had a dress on like a lady.'

'You're playing with yourself again, Darren,' Elsie accused.

Darren spat at her and lunged out with his fist.

'Shut up, both of you!' Martin ordered. 'D'you think it matters about Sarah being on the telly?' he asked Mr Godfrey.

Mr Godfrey had been worrying over that himself. 'No, I don't think so. There was no sign of Darren in any of the pictures, thank goodness, and Sarah only appeared very briefly. If anyone *should* recognise her they'd simply think she was one of the demonstrators. She was in the middle of them, after all.'

'What'll happen now—about this place, I mean?'

'I imagine they'll close it up for good. They won't keep it going now that everyone knows about it. They'll clear everything out and leave an empty shell.'

'We won't be able to live here any more then?'

'No, I'm afraid not.'

They were silent for a while, taking in the catastrophe.

'Are there any other places like this one?' asked Sarah.

'Good question,' Mr Godfrey commented. 'Yes, Sarah, there are. But I don't know where they are.'

'Isn't there some way of finding out?' asked Martin.

Mr Godfrey smiled. 'No, the locations are all Top Secret. They're not on any—' He broke off, staggered by the simplicity of an idea that had occurred to him. 'But they *are*!' he went on. 'They're marked on the scientist's plotting screen. Come on!'

He led them along the tunnel to the Operations Room and into the scientists room attached to it.

'But surely if the locations are marked up,' said Martin, 'those people who came in here today would have seen them and they wouldn't be secret anymore.'

'Ah, but it's not that simple,' Mr Godfrey told him. 'I'll show you why.' He went to the big six-foot-square glass screen in the centre of the room.

'The scientific officer stands this side,' Mr Godfrey explained to Martin, 'and draws his predictions on the glass with a felt-tipped pen. The clerks sit the other side plotting the nuclear bursts and the damage reports. Now, if you look closely, you'll see symbols marked on the screen at various places. One of these symbols represents other underground headquarters like this one.'

Martin peered at the screen. 'There are funny marks everywhere.'

'That's right. Hospitals, depots, rest centres . . . there are signs for all of them.'

'Then how can we tell which—'

'I'll give you a clue.' Mr Godfrey smiled, pleased with his own cleverness. 'Do you see these lines engraved on the glass—running from side to side and top to bottom—dividing it into squares?'

Martin examined them and studied the figures at the end of the lines. 'It's the National Grid, isn't it? The same as on maps?'

'That's right!' He was delighted that Martin remembered the map-reading he'd taught him in their early days in the bunker and when they went for walks on the Downs. 'Now, we know the position of *this* headquarters, don't we? So we can work out its grid reference from a map. We look at that reference point on the screen here and see what symbol we find marked. That will tell us the symbol for an underground headquarters. Then all we have to do is to look for other symbols the same, read off their grid reference from the screen, reverse the process and find that point on a map.'

'Gobbledygook,' said Sarah, who had been trying to follow the explanation.

'It's not!' said Martin hotly. 'It's jolly smart. *I* can understand it.'

They could find only two other sites in the area of country covered by the scientist's screen. Mr Godfrey settled on the one in East Anglia. He'd heard about that one when he'd been in Civil Defence himself, although he'd not then known its exact location. He knew it had been purpose-built and wasn't a conversion job like Warren Row. Because of this it had large air shafts with filters across the outside to trap radioactive dust particles. If the filter was removed, a child or a small adult could crawl along one of those shafts and gain access to the place. He wouldn't be able to get in himself but it didn't matter because he'd decided he wasn't going with them.

Mr Godfrey had done a great deal of thinking over the last day or two. Cooped up with the children in that small hideout in the chalk, forced into the closest intimacy with their basic natural functions, he'd asked himself: What on earth am I doing here? To them it had all been a bit of a lark; but he was too old for this kind of game. His time with the children had been a sort of long escape, rather like having a nervous breakdown and entering a mental hospital for a while. A break from the world outside, surrounded by people with worse problems than your own until the time came to face the world once more.

He'd had his break and he was ready to face life again. The demonstration he'd witnessed had given him fresh heart too. If you didn't agree with something you stood up to it and fought! That ridiculous shoplifting charge he'd have to face—that was nothing to be frightened of. It wasn't the end of the world, even if he was convicted. And he wasn't gong to be pushed around by Mrs Godfrey any more either. Perhaps some of the blame was his for the way things were between them. He should have been firmer with her. She'd have respected him for it. He squared his shoulders. It wasn't too late to change the situation.

He'd grown fond of the children, of course—even Darren—and they'd probably saved his sanity when he was confused and upset. He was glad he'd been able to help them. They'd made him feel wanted and important when no one else seemed to have any use for him. They'd taught him things he hadn't known about life and, despite the enormous age gap, in a curious way they'd taught him about people. He'd always be grateful and he'd never forget them. But they didn't need him now. Their father would be out of prison soon and they'd be all right then. He wouldn't tell them yet that he was separating from them. He'd see them safely on their way and then part quickly and cleanly.

'There's a snag,' Martin was saying. 'We're out of money.'

'I have a pound or two left,' said Mr Godfrey. He would give them the rest of his money, keeping only enough to get him back home.

'We need more than that,' said Martin. 'There's money for fares—I doubt if we can hitch-hike all the way. And we'll have to spend a night somewhere—we can't sleep rough this weather.'

'I can get money,' Elsie volunteered.

'Yes and we know *how!*' said Martin. 'Last summer you went round the parks showing your knickers to dirty old men for 50p.'

'I only *showed*,' she said defensively. 'There was another girl who pulled hers *down*. She got a pound a time.'

'That's disgusting?' said Sarah, scandalised.

'Anyway, we're having none of that this time,' Martin said. '*I'll* find a way of providing the money.'

'You may not have much time,' Mr Godfrey warned. 'There could be engineers in any day to begin dismantling this place.'

160

Eighteen

Saul Harrison gazed out of the big bay window of his house in one of the Nash Terraces overlooking Regent's Park. It was dark and the street lamps threw soft light along the terrace. Saul was fond of those lamps—they were so different from the hard, modern lights that illuminated most of London—and he found it soothing to rest his eyes upon them and let his thoughts wander.

Dinner was over and in a moment or two he would make an excuse to his wife and daughter and withdraw to his study. There he could plug in the video recorder to the television and view the videotape he'd brought home that evening. There was nothing unusual in that. His firm had been experimenting for some time with equipment to link microprocessors and videotapes and Louise and Dena were used to him trying out new gimmicks at home. He often brought home videofilms but what was different this evening was that he wanted to view in private. This was a rather special piece of videofilm and, although it was certainly not pornographic, he'd borne it home like a guilty schoolboy hiding a dirty book from his parents.

The woman had telephoned his office the previous morning. She'd refused to tell his secretary who she was or what she wanted.

His secretary said plaintively: 'She says to tell you it's Jean from Hackney and you'll understand.'

161

'It's a personal call,' Saul told her. 'Put her through.'

The coarse, slightly husky voice breathed in his ear. 'It's Jean, remember me?'

Her voice quickened his senses, just as it had in the flat. He remembered her untidyness, the underwear lying about, those sharp little breasts under the tight black dress.

He gave a nervous laugh. 'Yes, of course.'

'I thought you would,' she said pertly. There was a pause. Then: 'Is your *friend*—' she put emphasis on the word, '—still interested in information?'

Obviously she hadn't believed his story that his enquiries about the Pace family were on behalf of a friend.

'He might be,' said Saul cautiously. 'It depends on what the information is.'

'It's about one of the Pace kids. Sarah. Would it be worth a tenner to know where she was last Sunday?'

His daughter. Saul tensed slightly. 'Yes, it would.'

'Did you see all the fuss on the telly about that secret place in Berkshire the Nukes got into?'

'I saw something about it on the news, yes.'

'Well, Sarah was there. In the news, as large as life. They were talking to that old twit of a priest and there she was, in her Girl Guide outfit, right in the front of the picture! I nearly died laughing. It was only for a moment, but she was there all right.'

Saul waited. She'd finished, however.

'Is that all?' he asked, disappointed.

'It's something, isn't it? I mean, she must've been on the march, mustn't she?'

A useless piece of knowledge. Still, that wasn't the woman's fault. 'Yes, thank you.' He felt he should say more. 'Has there been any news of your little boy—' he fumbled for the name, '—Darren?'

'No.' She sounded surprised that he should ask. 'I've given up. I can't mope forever. They aren't going to find him—leastways not alive.' Again there was that lack of warmth in her voice when she spoke about the child, which had jarred on him at the flat.

'I'll mail the ten pounds to you,' he said.

'You could bring it yourself,' she suggested, her voice dropping into the seductive tone she'd used on him in the flat.

'I'll think about it.' He broke the connection.

His first thought was not to bother further with what Jean had told him. It wasn't exactly earth-shattering. His illegitimate daughter had appeared among a crowd of demonstrators, that was all. But then, as so often with Saul, his curiosity began to gnaw at him. What did this daughter of his look like? She was thirteen. Was she plain? Ugly? Was she pretty? Sexy, even? He grinned. The last, faded photograph of her in his deed box was of a toothy four-year-old. She might have turned out a right little raver, this love-child. He decided he wanted to know; wanted to see what she looked like.

He buzzed his secretary. 'Find out if we've any News-freaks in the office. I'd like to borrow a videotape of last Sunday's television news. Either Channel will do.'

Several of his staff, like him, had video recorders at home. But he'd probably be unlucky. No one taped the news—it wasn't something people wanted to watch a second time as a rule. Someone had, however, and Saul had experienced a tingle of anticipation when he'd been handed the cassette that morning and put it in his brief case to bring home.

He had the same feeling now as he said to his wife: 'I'm just going to run through an old tape on the set in the study, Louise. Shan't be long.'

She nodded, uninterested. Dena asked: 'Is it anything exciting, Daddy?'

'No, darling, it's only an old newsreel.'

He had to view it in private. He'd need to run the

videotape more than once in order to select and then hold the individual frames in which Sarah appeared; and he couldn't do that without some awkward questions being asked if Louise or Dena were present.

In the study he loaded the tape, switched on the set and sat down in an armchair to watch, holding the control module in his hand. He pressed the 'roll forward' button until the tape reached the beginning of Sunday's news. The newscaster introduced the item on the Aldermaston march and the picture changed to scenes of the marchers assembling outside Reading station. There were shots of the progress of the march and then a dramatic sequence as the marchers approached the compound in the woods and the police car raced to intercept them. The cameraman with a telephoto lens, or perhaps the film editor later, had managed to make the white Rover, approaching at speed through the trees, look like a charging rhinoceros as it bumped and bounded over the uneven ground.

Suddenly the sequence cut to a close-up of Father Black sitting on a table swinging his legs. Almost at once a girl's head obtruded into the picture. Saul stopped the tape, tracked back and moved forward a frame at a time to the one in which the girl first appeared. He leaned forward. This must be Sarah. Guide's uniform, as Jean had said. Saul examined the face. Serious, innocent, but she was a looker, definitely a good-looker. He moved the tape on slowly until he came to the last shots of Sarah before the camera moved away from her. She was stretching over, one leg in the air, to something or somebody, out of the picture. He studied the long, slim legs critically. She was not only a good-looker, she had good legs too.

The study door had opened without him hearing it. 'Daddy, you old lecher!' Dena exclaimed, closing the door. 'What would Mummy say?' She giggled and came forward to stand beside him. 'Who is she?'

He took her hand and pulled her down on to his

lap. 'How should I know? I'm just experimenting with the colour contrast of some new tape we're using.'

She gave a snort of disbelief. 'Liar!' she cried in mock anger. 'You're drooling over that girl.' She looked at the screen. 'Her legs are too thin. They're not as nice as mine, are they?' she asked coquettishly.

He slipped a hand under her dress and squeezed her knee. 'No, not nearly as nice. Now sit still while I look at the rest of this tape.'

He ran through the whole cassette, stopping now and again and pretending to criticise the quality, to allay Dena's suspicions. It took some time but he was content to sit there in the dim light of the screen, her soft body fitting the shape of his lap and her thighs pressing through the thin cotton dress. His thoughts wandered. Another daughter. He'd never thought of Sarah as that. She was out there somewhere. Cool, golden-haired . . . distant. Dena was here with him, though. Warm, dark . . . cuddly. He hugged her to him with a sigh of happiness.

The demand that Saul had been dreading, but which he'd convinced himself would not, after all, be made, came the next evening.

Dena answered the telephone and he listened with amusement as she put on a studied, grown-up voice.

'This is his daughter, Dena Harrison, speaking. Can I help you?' She turned to Saul with her hand over the mouthpiece. 'There's a rather rude person on the telephone, Daddy. He won't give his name. He says he must speak to Mr Saul Harrison.' She handed him the receiver and flounced out of the room.

'Yes? Harrison speaking,' he said curtly.

'You have a daughter called Sarah.' It was a statement not a question and the tone was hostile.

Saul's hand shook slightly. 'Who is this?'

'Next time I'll tell that girl who answered she's got a sister.'

'What do you want?' he asked harshly.

'Fifty pounds.'

He couldn't believe he'd heard right. This was an absurdly small sum for a blackmail demand. 'Would you repeat that?' Perhaps he meant fifty pounds a week.

'I said fifty pounds.' The voice sounded less assured. 'I want it tomorrow.'

Saul hesitated and then asked: 'Is this a once-only payment?'

'What's that mean?' The voice became even more uncertain.

'Well, are you going to be back next week for more, or next month or—'

'No! This'll be the lot.' The reply was quick, almost panicky.

The caller was clearly an amateur but he didn't seem to be an ordinary blackmailer. Saul was bewildered. He'd worried himself sick just after Christmas, expecting to be screwed for hundreds, maybe thousands of pounds and now he was being asked for *fifty*. It was farcical. Farce or not though, the threat to his family was real enough.

'Very well. Where do we meet?'

'We don't. You put the money in an envelope and I'll tell you where to leave it. Get a paper and pencil and write this down.'

Saul wrote out the instructions carefully and repeated them back. He tried to prolong the conversation but the caller brought it to an abrupt end.

'Tomorrow. Twelve o'clock.' The line went dead.

Terry looked into Butch Fearon's cold eyes and trembled inwardly. He lifted the pint glass of beer that Butch had set in front of him and took a long, slow mouthful while he looked furtively around the bar seeking in vain an excuse to escape.

'The way I see it, Terry,' Butch was saying, 'we start at the place where we saw 'em before . . . in them woods at Warren Row.'

'But they won't be there now,' Terry said nervously. Being close to Butch, his thatch of new black hair making him seem odder than ever, was making Terry twitch.

'I bin thinking about that,' said Butch, 'and I reckon they live around there. Remember how them kids was dressed?'

Every scene was etched in Terry's memory. Every scene from when they'd sneaked into the wood to the moment they'd deposited Butch's burned and unconscious body beside the telephone box and dialled 999. He'd never ever forget the smell of burnt human flesh.

'I remember.'

'Think about what they was wearing.'

Terry stared at him in astonishment. Deciding it was best to humour him he said: 'Well, the tiddler—the one who disappeared—was in a light blue dress and the other one—' he closed his eyes, recalling Sarah '—dark-blue skirt and jumper.'

'Right. What's missing?'

Terry stole a cautious glance at him. Butch was bats. Did he mean—

'*They wasn't wearing coats*, you dum-dum! It was cold, right? Middle of winter, right? And they didn't have no coats on!' He leaned back with an air of triumph.

Terry couldn't see the point. 'So?'

'So they must live somewhere *close*,' Butch said patiently. 'And that's why you and me's starting right there.'

'Oh, yeh. I see.' Terry looked down at his hands. No way was he going to Warren Row with Butch Fearon, no matter if he was given a hammering for refusing. He

167

knew something Butch didn't. Last Sunday when Terry had been watching his favourite cartoon on TV he'd strayed over into the beginning of the news. The name 'Warren Row' had caught his ear and he'd turned his attention to the news item. He'd followed the scenes of the marchers running through the woods—even thought he'd spotted the very place where they'd caught that blonde piece. Then, a few seconds later, he'd been staggered to see Sarah herself, down in the bunker with the demonstrators.

Perhaps Butch was right and she *did* live around there. If so Butch would find her. Do all those things to her he'd kept on about in hospital. His mind would blow once he had his hands on her. He'd kill her for sure. Terry was certain of that.

'No, Butch, leave me outta this.' The words came jerkily from his mouth. Now Butch would haul him outside and beat Hell out of him.

The merciless eyes fastened on his face. In a flat voice Butch Fearon said:

'You know what she done, Terry, the little bitch. You was there. I'm all knotted up inside thinking about it and I won't have no peace till I've sorted her out. She won't feel like living when I've done with her. She ain't strutting around all pretty and whole while I'm—' his voice cracked with fury. '—while I'm like this!'

'Butch, it was a terrible thing she done, but I ain't getting tied in with no killing—and that's what it'll come to.' He averted his face afraid to meet those dead eyes.

'You already are, Terry,' Butch said softly.

'What d'ya mean?' Terry gawped at him.

'That ole man we done over at Baker Street that time. He snuffed it. Same night.'

'That ain't true!' Terry cried hotly. 'You never said nothing before!'

'It's true. It was in the paper. Think I'd make it up? Get

someone to check for you—seeing as you can't read,' he sneered.

Terry swallowed. '*You* was the one kept putting the boot in and stomping his chest. I only kicked his arse.'

'Try telling that to the law. You're in it—up to here.' He made a movement across his throat with his finger.

'*Oh, Christ!*' Terry let out a groan and lowered his face, ashamed of the tears of fright gathering in his eyes. Fearfully, he whispered: 'Leave me outta this, Butch . . . *please!*'

Butch glared at the bowed head for a while. Then his lip curled.

'Yeh, I reckon I'd better. You wouldn't be no good. You'd be pissing yourself with fright when it came to doing anything, you poxy little bastard.'

Grateful to be let off and relieved that he wasn't getting a beating after all, Terry told Butch about Sarah and the demonstration in the underground headquarters. Later that night he was to sit in his bedroom agitatedly biting his nails over being accessory to another murder and wondering what to do about it. Butch's slow brain digested the information.

At last he said: 'It all fits.' He looked pleased. 'Didn't you say there was an ole man with 'em when you followed 'em that night?'

'Yeh, that's right.'

'Well, places like that has to have a caretaker. I reckon the ole geezer's a caretaker and them kids is his. Or p'raps he's their grandad. I'm sure they live in them woods somewhere—maybe in the bunker itself.' His eyes gleamed. 'She's there, I know she is, Terry.' He became suddenly cheerful. 'Drink up! We'll have another jar.' He belched and smacked his lips. 'I could drink a brewery dry after all that time in hospital without it.'

Later, he said, 'There's two things you can get me Terry. I need wheels—nothing flashy to attract attention

—just a reliable motor. Tomorrow, right?'

Terry nodded. Butch leaned forward. 'And the other thing—' He put his mouth to Terry's ear and told him his sordid requirement. Terry's mouth opened in surprise. He looked into the granite eyes. They were daring him to comment. He shivered and said nothing.

In the bunker at Warren Row Mr Godfrey and the children had been having a miserable time. They had re-rigged the alarm buzzer and hardly a morning or afternoon passed without its sounding. Each time it sent them running to the chalk cave to hide until whoever had entered the bunker had departed again. Often this was hours later. There was a succession of intruders: officials from innumerable government departments with a finger in the decision to close the headquarters; and electricians, engineers and the like.

'Up and down! Up and down!' Elsie grumbled. 'Always moving. It's worse'n when we was on the Tube.'

Then, for her, came the final disaster. After one such visit she came running from the Recreation Room.

'They've taken the telly!' she wailed. 'We can't stay here without a telly.'

'We'll be all right until they cut off the electricity or take away the food stores,' Mr Godfrey said soothingly.

'The washing-machine has gone too,' Sarah reported. 'And the tumble dryer. I can't keep our clothes clean anymore.'

'We'll leave tomorrow,' said Martin. 'If we have to, we'll hitch-hike and sleep out.'

Nineteen

Saul Harrison arrived long before the appointed time at the spot where he'd been instructed to leave the money. Yesterday evening, when he'd been writing down the instructions, he'd suppressed his exclamation of surprise on being told that the telephone box where he was to deposit the envelope was a few hundred yards from the village of Warren Row. Was it simply an extraordinary coincidence that this was also near the location of last week-end's rumpus in which Sarah had apparently taken part? No, there had to be a connection; yet he didn't see what it could be. The voice on the telephone had been male, but whether a man's or a youth's he couldn't tell. In any case the caller had probably disguised his voice.

Saul was convinced that either the Pace family—or someone very close to them—was behind the affair. Fifty pounds was neither here nor there to him but he intended to make sure this would be the only payment and to find out who was doing this to him.

He parked at the pub in Warren Row and carried out a discreet but thorough reconnaissance of the area on foot. Afterwards he sat in the pub sipping lager until it was 11.30. Then he left Warren Row and drove on to Holly Cross and down to Wargrave, circling back to the A4 so as to approach the rendezvous at twelve o'clock as though he'd come straight from London.

There were no houses in the vicinity of the telephone box and it was unoccupied when he stopped beside it. Had there been anyone inside his instructions were to wait until they left. Saul went inside, opened up the S-Z Directory and pinned the envelope containing ten £5 notes to the first page of the S entries. He closed the volume and let it fall back in position under the shelf.

As he drove away he kept observation in his rear mirror but saw nobody. A few hundred yards along the road, up a slight rise and out of sight from the telephone kiosk, was the pub that he'd left half an hour before. Parking the car again he snatched up his binoculars, crossed the road, and ran along the public footpath to Knowl Hill to the observation point in the hedge that he'd selected earlier. His watch showed four minutes past twelve. Had the money been collected already? He focused the binoculars on the telephone box.

The only person in sight was a small girl in a grey coat. Saul watched her approach the box and tug open the door with an effort. He smiled and lowered the glasses. She wasn't his blackmailer.

Almost at once she left the box again. Quickly he raised the binoculars. Through the glass side of the kiosk he could see one of the Directories lying open on the shelf. The girl was walking away down the road. Saul swore. The blackmailer had adopted the trick of using a child to pick up the money. He raced back to the car, started it up and roared after her. She was skipping unconcernedly along the side of the road as he overtook her and braked to a stop. Saul wound down his window. He was not sure at this moment whether she was an innocent go-between or if she was involved in some way. Feeling self-conscious and slightly foolish he called out:

'Where are you going to, little girl?'

She halted and squinted at him out of almond-shaped eyes. Her clothes were clean but well-worn and her black hair was badly cut. Saul thought she was about nine or ten.

'Well, come on,' he prompted, when she didn't answer. 'Where are you off to?'

'I'm not allowed to talk to strangers,' she said primly and walked on.

'Just a moment!' he called sharply, getting out of the car. 'You took an envelope from the telephone box back there and I want to know where you're going with it.'

She bolted like a rabbit. She zig-zagged, white socks twinkling, as Saul chased after her. If she'd run into the woods he'd have had trouble catching her but she didn't and it was an unfair contest. Her small legs were no match against his long ones on the open road. He grabbed her as she reached a wide, padlocked gate across a track into the woods. He gripped her arm and she froze, not struggling.

'Now, what's your name?' he demanded. There was no response.

'Where do you live? I want to speak to your parents.'

She stayed silent, her small chest pumping up and down as she began to recover her breath.

'All right, then,' he said in exasperation, 'I'm taking you to the police station.' If he expected that to frighten her, he was disappointed.

'OK,' she said indifferently.

He led her back to the car and looked up and down the road, expecting someone to jump out and claim her. No one did. Opening the car door to put her in, he made another attempt. 'The policemen will be very cross, you know,' he told her. 'Why don't you tell me where you live, eh?'

She gave him a disdainful look and clambered in. He turned the car round and drove back to the telephone box. Keeping a sharp eye on the girl in case she made a run for it again, he entered the box. The Directory lying open was the S-Z volume and the envelope was gone. Since she wasn't holding it in her hand and she hadn't had a chance to pass it to anyone, it had to be on her somewhere.

He tried once more to scare her as he drove slowly towards the village. 'Well, it's the police station now,' he said sternly. 'A policewoman will search you and find you've got fifty pounds of mine.'

'What you gonna tell the cops?' she asked.

'That you've stolen my money, of course.'

She cocked an eye at him. 'I'll tell them you've done things to me in your car,' she threatened. '*Bad* things.'

He swerved, then regained control. Triumphantly, she added:

'I'll say that's what you gave me the money for!'

He braked to a halt outside the pub. She'd defeated him, this chit of a girl. But he was unwilling simply to let her walk off without finding out anything at all. Bluff and threats hadn't worked. Clearly he'd made a tactical error. He contemplated her open, innocent face. Perhaps she could be sweet-talked into giving him information. Also, if he hung on to her, someone ought to be worried that she hadn't shown up and come looking for her.

He put on a friendly smile. 'What would you say to a drink of orange? Or a lemonade?'

She thought about it. 'OK.'

He turned into the car park for the third time and she hopped out and followed him into the pub. There was a Family Room for children at the rear. It was empty.

'What would you like?' he asked her as the barman poked his head through the hatch in the wall from another bar.

She reeled off her requirements like a shopping list. 'A bottle of coke, two straws and two packets of cheese and onion crisps.'

'And a lager for me,' Saul told the barman.

'Not sure about cheese and onion, dear,' said the

174

barman as he served the drinks. 'I'll have to look.'

Two bench seats jutted out from the wall with a table between them. Clutching her bottle of coke with the straws sticking out of the neck, the girl slid along one of the seats. Saul sat down beside her. She took a long, deep, draught through the straws and then expelled her breath in a loud, vulgar gasp.

The barman reappeared. 'Here you are, dear, two cheese and onion.' He planted the packets on the hatch shelf.

She stood up to push past Saul and go to the hatch and he saw an opportunity to retrieve the envelope and the money. If he whipped it off her he would be in a better bargaining position. As she bent over, squeezing between him and the table, he swiftly patted her coat pocket. Nothing. A dress pocket perhaps? He fumbled under her coat.

'Hey! Watch it!' she said sharply. 'Keep your hands to yourself!' She extricated herself quickly from between his knees.

'I only patted you.'

But Elsie was experienced from her time on the London Tube and especially from travelling in the rush-hour.

'I know the difference between a pat on the bottom and a feel-up!' she snapped. 'And that was a goddamned feel-up!'

She held out her hand for money for the crisps. He had no small change and he gave her a pound from his wallet. When she returned she moved pointedly along the other side of the table. She put his change in her pocket and sat opposite him placidly chewing her crisps.

While he was wondering how to proceed, a youth with carrot-coloured hair put his head round the door. His face showed sudden relief when he saw the girl. With a wary eye on Saul he advanced into the room. 'All right, Elsie,' he said, 'cut along. I'll handle this.'

She looked up. 'I haven't finished me crisps,' she complained.

'Take them with you,' he ordered, and now Saul recognised the voice from yesterday's telephone call.

'OK Martin.' She carefully folded over the opened packet and placed it in her coat pocket. She reached out and picked up the other packet. I'll give this one to Darren,' she said grandly.

Names began dropping into slots in Saul's memory. Names from long ago. Elsie . . . Martin—Eastbourne. That mewling baby in the cot beside the bed.

'You're Martin!' he said incredulously. 'Carol's boy. You're Martin Pace.'

Elsie was sliding out from the table. 'Ta-ta,' she said, making for the door.

Saul half-stood. 'Hang on. She's walking off with my money.'

Martin's tall frame blocked him. 'You agreed to pay,' he said flatly. 'We made a bargain.' Elsie slipped out of the door.

'Yes, but—' Saul sat down again. He wasn't really bothered about the money. He was more concerned to find out where he stood with this lad.

'I think you and I should have a little talk,' said Saul. 'Let me get you a drink.'

'No thanks,' Martin said curtly.

'Oh come on. We aren't exactly enemies.'

'Cider, then,' Martin said grudgingly.

When they were seated with their drinks Saul said:

'You know, you'd be in a lot of trouble if I went to the police.'

'So would you. I saw you snatch little Elsie off the road and push her into your car. I was too far away to stop you.'

'But I wasn't going to do her any harm!'

'The police won't believe that.'

Saul took a mouthful of his drink. 'How did you find us?'

'I hared after the car and after you'd stopped at the 'phone box and dawdled up the hill, I wasn't far behind. I saw you park at the pub and I just looked in all the bars until I found you.'

Saul studied Martin. Despite his hostility the boy seemed harmless enough. He leaned towards him. 'Well, now, what do you think you're up to?' Martin looked down and said nothing. 'Blackmail,' Saul went on, then saw the boy flinch. '*Blackmail*,' he repeated, 'because that's what it is, is a very serious matter.'

'We *need* the money. Sarah—all of us. She's your daughter and you've never given her *anything*!' The blue eyes blazed angrily. 'You didn't help mum one penny with Sarah when she was a baby.'

Taken aback Saul said defensively, 'Your mother wouldn't let me.'

'I don't believe that!' Martin retorted hotly. 'You were just too mean!'

I don't want your money, damn you! Carol had said *And don't you ever send any or I'll post it straight back to your wife!*

'I know better than you, Martin,' Saul said quietly. He made a quick calculation. 'You were about three years old when Sarah was born. How could you know anything of what happened at that time?'

'I have my mother's diary.'

'*Diary!*' Saul boggled at him. An icy hand gripped his heart. A *diary*. Intimate details of their affair.

'I've read it too.' Martin's voice was bitter. 'She was crazy about you, you rotten bastard.'

Saul winced at the venom in the boy's voice. Carol had never mentioned a diary. How could she have been so stupid. How—?

'How do you come to have her diary?'

177

Martin didn't answer for a while. Then he shrugged his shoulders and said:

'When mum was in hospital after she'd had Elsie, she—' He stopped and drew a breath. '—she knew she was dying. She told me there was a little book of hers which could make Dad and all of us very unhappy. I was only a kid—same age as Elsie now—I didn't really understand. She made me promise to burn it. But I couldn't find it. There wasn't a hiding place where she said. She must have been wandering in her mind and didn't tell me right.' He looked away. 'And then she was dead and I couldn't do what she asked.'

His face closed up in pain and Saul had a momentary vision of a small boy's misery: the anguish of his mother's death and of knowing that he'd failed her. Martin continued:

'Last summer, when Dad was sent to prison, we stripped the flat before we left and down behind a partition in a cupboard, I found mum's little book—it was a five-year diary. She'd started it when she left school. I read it and found out about Sarah.'

'Sarah doesn't—? I mean, you haven't—?'

'No, I haven't told her and I'm not going to. Nor Dad. He still thinks Sarah's his. Mum was right. It would make them very unhappy to know.'

'And you?'

'Doesn't make much difference to me. We had the same mum. She's still my sister.' He said it with a note of pride.

'I suppose my address was in the diary. You found I still lived there and you decided to screw some money out of me.'

'I told you. We *need* the money. You won't miss fifty pounds.'

'Shouldn't you destroy the diary now, though? It's what your mother wanted you to do, after all,' Saul said persuasively.

'It doesn't matter now. You needn't worry, I won't bother you again if that's what you're afraid of.'

Maybe not, but someone else might, Saul thought grimly. Suppose the husband, Joe Pace read the diary one day? It could make him vindictive. God! Suppose he went to Louise? *This is what your husband was up to with my wife.* Saul shuddered. Louise would cut him to ribbons even now, all these years after the affair. And she'd tell Dena about Sarah. The diary was the only evidence there was. If he could gain possession of it . . .

'Look here, Martin,' he said in a friendly voice, 'I'd like to buy that diary of your mother's. For Old Time's Sake, you understand?'

'It's *private!*' said Martin, horrified.

'Well, then, I'll burn it without reading it. Tell you what, we'll burn it together. How's that? I'll give you a hundred pounds and we'll burn the diary.'

'No,' Martin said obstinately. 'I'm keeping it. It's the only thing of my mother's I have left.'

'Two hundred pounds then,' Saul said, his temper rising.

Martin shook his head.

Fuming, Saul searched for a way to pressure the boy. He'd have no peace of mind while that diary was around. Something Elsie had said linked up with a suspicion that had been forming in his mind.

'Your Dad's in prison, isn't he?' Martin nodded.

'I suppose you and Sarah and Elsie are all together somewhere?'

'Ye-es.'

'And *Darren*,' Saul shot at him. 'Is *he* with you?'

'No!' The boy's eyes widened in alarm. He tried to recover himself. 'Who is Darren?'

'Don't give me that!' Saul rasped. 'I've spoken to Darren's mother, Jean. I *know* who Darren is, and so do you. That was a mistake on your part to pretend you don't know who he is. And Elsie let it out when she said she'd give Darren her other bag of crisps.'

'You're talking rubbish,' Martin blustered. 'That's another boy she knows called Darren.'

Saul drained his glass and stood up. He didn't want to allow time for argument. 'I'll return tomorrow with two hundred pounds. You bring that diary—meet me here— or I'll be on the 'phone to the police.'

He paused at the door. 'There was no need for you to have sent that note at Christmas—that was a lousy trick.'

'Note?' Martin seemed genuinely astonished. 'I didn't send you any note.'

'Oh, to Hell with you!' Saul said impatiently and stalked out.

'Who *was* that man?' Elsie asked. She was sitting on a tree stump near the shaft into the bunker, where Martin had told her to wait.

'Just a man,' he replied. Earlier that morning he'd taken her aside. 'I want you to do something, Elsie, and I don't want you to tell anyone else about it.' She'd nodded eagerly. Elsie loved keeping secrets. Martin had explained that all she had to do was to walk to the telephone box and collect an envelope.

'Is it an important envelope, Martin?'

'Yes, very. Don't lose it.'

He'd told the others that he had to go into the village for something and that he was taking Elsie for company. He'd kept well away down the road out of sight while she carried out her mission.

'Where's the envelope, then?' he now asked.

She stood up and lifted up her coat and dress. She yanked her vest out of the elastic waist of her pants and a buff-coloured envelope fell to the ground.

'Well done, Elsie,' said Martin.

Twenty

Butch Fearon drove slowly along Warren Row Road. He'd passed the telephone box where, weeks before, Sid and Terry had deposited him to await the ambulance. Now he was looking for the place where he'd spotted the two girls in the woods that day after leaving the pub.

The afternoon was grey and dusk was already near. There was no one about as he left the car and entered the wood. He walked backwards and forwards traversing, and gradually penetrating deeper, until he found the square concrete shape in the ground, hidden by the undergrowth. Butch grunted with satisfaction. This was the drain or sewer, or whatever it was, where she'd gone down. He tried to raise the steel cover. It was secured from below.

'Everybody ready?' the children were ready to leave the bunker and Mr Godfrey watched Martin make a check of the haversacks as they hoisted them on to their shoulders. He was reminded of their journey here weeks ago. Same faces—well, one more, of course—same haversacks, same sense of setting out for the unknown.

'Come along then.' He tried to sound cheerful.

'Bye-bye home,' Elsie said sadly.

'I don't wanna go!' Darren howled, wrestling with Sarah.

'Hush,' she said soothingly. 'We'll find another nice place, you'll see.' Wistfully, she gazed round. 'I liked it here,' she said.

'Come on, Sis.' Martin put his arm round her.

Mr Godfrey's feelings were mixed. He shared the children's sadness at leaving Warren Row. His stay here had been an interlude—a brief escape—a small island of happiness in his life. He would rearrange his affairs when he returned home. Make things different . . . better. He wondered if the children would mind very much when he told them he wasn't coming with them. The yearning to stay with them was strong. Perhaps he . . .? No, he mustn't start wavering.

Martin was in the lead as they crossed the Plant-Room and entered the short passage to the bottom of the escape shaft. Suddenly he turned round and pushed them back.

'Someone's coming!' he hissed. 'Someone's coming down the shaft!'

'No one comes in that way,' said Mr Godfrey. 'They can't. It's bolted.'

'Well, someone *is*!' Martin insisted in a whisper. And now they could hear the scrape of feet on the iron rungs.

'Quick! Into the hideout, all of you and take the bags,' urged Mr Godfrey. In seconds, adopting the routine they'd followed so many times before, they were safely inside with the pegboard in place.

Butch Fearon reached the bottom of the shaft and stood listening. He'd levered open the lid with a jack handle from the car, bursting the bolt from its housing. When he'd peered down the shaft into the gloom the scene had come back to him as vivid as the moment it happened. The girl down there pointing something up at him. The sudden bang, the force of the impact and the blaze of light. Then flames . . . scorching cloth . . . screaming agony . . . passing out. *She'd* done that to him. He saw the door in the side of the shaft and tried the handle. To his surprise it opened. Beyond was a chalk-walled passage.

Cautiously, he moved along the passage and through the open doors of the airlock. He blinked his eyes as he emerged into the well-lit Plant-Room. He stood still, listening again. The place was silent. As he shambled towards the door at the other end of the room a spot of bright colour caught his attention and he changed direction. Lying on the floor below where a piece of hardboard was fixed to the wall, was something small and red. He picked it up. It was a child's glove. Butch stood holding the glove, his slow brain working at the problem and his moronic face creased with effort. He bent down and stared at the hardboard, trying to see through the holes.

Then, like some Frankenstein monster, he reached out, gripped the piece of board with his thick fingers and tore it from the wall. The light from the Plant-Room illuminated the square aperture in the chalk and he stooped and looked inside. He saw one terrified face. Then another. Then *hers*. Butch blinked, unable to believe his eyes. He must be dreaming. He shook his head and looked again. It was the girl all right. He'd been carrying that face in his mind's eye for weeks.

It was all he could do not to leap in there, take that slim white throat in his hands and squeeze the life out of her. She hadn't recognised him yet in the bad light and with his new growth of dark, curly hair. They were all there, crouching like rabbits waiting to be killed and skinned. Butch grinned evilly. Suddenly he reached inside, hooked an arm round the nearest, Darren, and plucked him out. Snatching his sheath knife from its holster on his belt he held it to Darren's neck.

'You lot do as you're told,' he snarled viciously, 'or I'll cut the kid's throat!' He jerked his head at Sarah. '*You!* Out here!'

As she began to clamber through the exit she looked up and recognised him.

'It's the Skinhead!' she shouted, trying to scramble inside again. Butch hurled Darren aside, seized her arm and dragged her out.

'You lot in there!' he yelled. 'Stay put or I'll carve the bitch up!'

Having her actually in his grasp at last, her body trembling against his own, was almost more than he could bear. He'd thought of this moment so many times and he longed to plunge the knife into her again and again. But first she had to be hurt. *Down there*. He rammed her to the wall.

'You move, I'll kill you!' he said through his teeth.

He replaced the knife in its holster. Sarah watched in paralysed horror as he brought the obscene object from his pocket and strapped it on to himself. Terry had purchased it for him in a Soho Sex Shop, choosing hurriedly, embarrassed by the rampant display of flesh-coloured monstrosities.

Staring wildly about her, Sarah saw Darren, agitated and gibbering, perched on top of the generator case behind Butch. Would he remember? He'd attacked Mr Godfrey at Christmas but would he respond now?

The Skinhead's hands were at the belt of her jeans.

'*Darren!* Darren *KILL!*' she screeched in a sub-human voice. 'Kill-kill-*KILL!*'

Darren leapt like a monkey on to Butch Fearon's back, gripping with his knees and flinging his arms tightly round the thick neck and under the chin. He locked his elbows together and squeezed with all his might. Full of hate, he was responding to Sarah's cry in the way he'd once been taught. Darren knew nothing of carotid arteries or that his armlock was compressing them. The deadly hold was denying blood and oxygen to the brain and, stunned with surprise, Butch began to lose consciousness almost at once.

He clawed ineffectually at Darren's coiled arms, bewildered by the rapid weakening of his muscles. In a change of tactics he dropped to his knees and rolled over on his back to crush the boy beneath his weight like an elephant dislodging a tiger from its back.

'Help!' Sarah cried. 'Oh, come quickly!'

Mr Godfrey scrambled from the hideout as Butch broke Darren's hold and staggered to his feet. Insane with frustrated rage he lifted the child by its ankles.

'NO!' Sarah screamed as he swung Darren backwards, about to dash his head against the wall.

Mr Godfrey threw himself forward. Caught off balance by the attack Butch stumbled and fell. As he went down his head struck the heavy generator casing and he lay motionless with Darren on top of him.

Martin and Elsie emerged from the cave, dragging the bundles and haversacks.

'Go quickly, all of you!' cried Mr Godfrey.

They hurried to the escape shaft with their possessions. He bent and removed the knife from its sheath and hurled it through the opening to the hideout. Butch began to stir and as Mr Godfrey followed the children he came to his feet, swearing and cursing and lumbered after him. In the narrow passage Mr Godfrey turned to brave the crazed Skinhead so as to gain time for the children to make their escape. He threw up his hands for protection as Butch tried to smash him aside and his glasses were broken and knocked from his face in the first blow. He could hardly see without them.

'Out of the way, you interfering old git!'

Mr Godfrey strove to keep his feet as the blows rained on him. He retreated to the foot of the shaft and seized the bottom rung, clenching his fingers round it. He clung there desperately, half-fainting, and preventing Butch from ascending. In a blind rage the Skinhead pounded him senseless until he sank to the floor. He stood on his chest and stomped savagely with his boots then kicked him aside and clambered up.

The children, slowed by their burdens, were still plainly in sight as they ran away through the darkening wood. He charged after them and was soon gaining on a screaming Elsie. But he only had eyes for Sarah's golden hair bobbing a few yards ahead of her. Butch was dimly aware of two dark figures racing to intercept him but his unhinged mind was closed to everything except the narrowing gap between him and his victim.

Not until strong arms brought him crashing down did he realise that the dark figures were policemen.

'Up on your knees, you bastard! Hands on the top of your head!'

Breathing hard the policemen stood up and looked around them. There was no sign of the children and the woods were silent again.

'Now where did *they* disappear to?' asked one. 'You'd have thought they'd come back when they saw us.'

They surveyed their kneeling captive. The disgusting phallus dangled grotesquely between his legs. One of the policemen leaned down and patted Butch's pockets. He found his wallet and straightened up, looking through it. The other policeman took a step forward, swung back his leg and crashed his boot into Butch's groin.

'You flaming pervert!' His voice shook.

They stood over him impassively as he writhed on the ground, waiting for him to recover. Then they would tell him why they were here and what they really wanted him for.

Terry had spent the morning havering and fretting. It was Butch who had done for the old man at Baker Street, not him or Sid. If Butch killed the girl—and Terry was afraid he would—he'd be involved in that too. *Murder*. He shivered. The more Terry thought about it the more it became clear to him that his only hope, the only way out for him, was to go to the police. He would explain about the old man and how he hadn't known he was dead until yesterday; and he'd warn them what Butch was up to.

Terry revealed everything to the police and he provided them with the description and number of the car he'd stolen for Butch. A message had been flashed to the Thames Valley police and a patrol car had been despatched and had found the stolen car. While the policemen were searching the woods for Butch Fearon, the fleeing children had suddenly appeared with Butch in pursuit.

Butch stopped moaning. 'On your feet!' He stood up and one of the policemen said in a formal voice:

'I have reason to believe that your name is Bertrand Fearon and that you are wanted by the Metropolitan Police in connection with the death of a man at Baker Street station last November . . .'

When he'd finished speaking the policeman waited for him to respond. Butch said nothing.

'Strong silent type, eh?' They laughed nastily.

They escorted him to their car. One of them pulled Butch's hands behind him. He thought he was to be handcuffed but his little fingers were seized and, with a sudden upward leverage, the policeman broke both his fingers at the joint.

'You won't be handling any more little girls for a while, Fearon,' he growled as he bundled a sobbing Butch Fearon into his car. He looked meaningfully at his companion.

'Resisting arrest. He tried to escape.'

'Yep, I saw him,' said the other policeman.

Twenty-one

'Why is Arnold crying?' asked Elsie.

'Because he's hurt,' said Sarah. 'He's in pain. *You* cry when you're hurt.' She was kneeling in the Plant-Room cradling Mr Godfrey's head in her lap.

From a distance, hidden among the trees, they had watched the policemen taking Butch Fearon away. They had doubled back and re-entered the shaft to find Mr Godfrey lying in a heap at the bottom. They had managed to manoeuvre him inside the Plant-Room and into the light.

His ribs were stoved in and he was breathing raggedly. As Sarah bent over him, her long hair caressing his face, he opened his eyes briefly and peered at her short-sightedly. Through a mist he saw grave blue eyes and flowing golden hair. His mind was years away in time and miles away in distance . . . out on the Metropolitan Line with his schoolgirl sweetheart.

'Chick?' he quavered.

'He thinks you're someone else,' said Martin. 'Who's Chick?'

'A girl he knew at school when he was a boy. He said I reminded him of her.'

'He's ever so old,' said Elsie. 'That's creepy.'

'No it's not. I think it's rather sweet.' Sarah bent and kissed the pale forehead.

Arnold Godfrey had drifted away again. Chick Courtney was holding her hand out to him. He took it and they both ran to the train. In the empty compartment she leaned forward and kissed him. He smiled happily.

'Look, he's smiling,' said Elsie. 'He must be better.'

Sarah gently lowered his head to the floor.

'He's dead,' she said.

Saul Harrison parked his car once more in the village of Warren Row and entered the pub. Martin was not in the Family Bar, nor was he in any of the other bars. Saul bought a drink and sat down to wait.

An hour later he accepted the fact that Martin Pace was not coming and that he was not going to hand over his mother's diary even for £200. Would the boy keep his word and not bother him again? Perhaps he would. He had that same air of honesty that his mother had had. Saul drove back to his office and replaced the money in the safe.

When he arrived home that evening Louise was waiting for him in the sitting-room, ominously upright in the Victorian button-back chair. It was her favourite piece of antique furniture and she always sat in it when she had something important to say. Most times it signified the beginning of a quarrel.

'Where's Dena?' he asked. Usually she greeted him as soon as he arrived home, pouring out her day to him in a stream of chatter.

'I've sent her to stay with a schoolfriend.'

'Oh? Why?' he demanded. Louise knew very well that he liked to be consulted before Dena stayed away from home.

'One reason, my dear Saul,' Louise said acidly, 'is that I don't want her to hear what I'm going to say to you.'

He sighed. He'd been right about her sitting in that chair. There was to be a row.

'What is it this time?' he asked in a tired voice.

She rose to her feet and flung on the table some things she'd been holding in her lap. Saul stared incredulously at the faded photographs and the typed report.

'You've been to my deed box! You've been through my papers!' he shouted angrily.

'Yes, I have.' Her voice was icy. 'I became sick of all those slushy letters you wrote to Dena when you were in America. Long, long letters. To me you sent *postcards*! I began to wonder about you, Saul . . . wondered what was so secret that you had to keep it locked up. So I took your precious box to a locksmith and had it opened and had him make me a key. I struck dirt, didn't I?'

'Louise, it was a long time ago,' he said wearily. 'And the laugh is I'm now being blackmailed over it.'

'Don't lie, Saul. You're not being blackmailed.'

'I tell you I *am*. I received a note at Christmas and—'

'*I* sent you that note.'

'*You?*'

'Yes, me. I wanted to see if you'd have the gumption to tell me about this yourself, if you were prodded. You hadn't. You're quite spineless, aren't you, Saul?' There was no malice in her voice, only curiosity. 'But then you always were, I suppose.'

'Louise, what do you want me to do? I can't wipe out the past. What do you want?'

'Want?' Her eyes were bright. 'I want a lot more attention from you. You've never put me first. At the beginning it was money. Oh, yes, you loved money more than me. Then it was that girl, Carol. Now it's Dena. You love *her* more than me!'

'Oh, for God's Sake, don't start quarrelling over Dena.'

'No, it won't be necessary. I'm sending her to boarding-school.'

'*No!*' The cry was wrung from him.

'Yes, Saul. Don't force me to tell her you've had another

daughter—a *love* daughter—all her life. Or perhaps you fancy the role of fallen idol. It would finish you with her, you know.'

He hung his head and didn't answer.

In the Plant-Room at Warren Row an engineer stared curiously at some letters cut into the chalk wall. He was waiting for his assistant to arrive so that they could begin dismantling the generators ready for removal. Had the initials been carved by some previous engineer, bored with his work? Chalk was soft, easy to dig into. Perhaps he'd inscribe his own name before they shut the place up for good.

'We must put *something*,' Sarah had said.

'Yes, but not much, we haven't time,' Martin told her.

They had dragged Mr Godfrey's body into the hideout and covered it with chalk rubble, bringing back some of the original debris from up in the woods. They had completely filled in the cave again, tamping down the chalk as they worked. Filling in the cave had been a lot easier than excavating it. Finally, they had fastened hard-board securely over the opening. Any curious person removing it would find only chalk rubble and even if they delved into the opening they would find nothing. Mr Godfrey lay deep inside against the far wall. 'What shall we put then?' asked Martin, a sharp piece of wood poised in his hand. 'His age? They always show that on grave-stones. How old was he d'you think?'

'Ninety,' said Elsie.

'He *wasn't*,' said Sarah. 'He wasn't that old.'

'Look, I'll just carve his initials and then ours.'

'I love Arnold,' said Darren.

'Let's write "with love" then,' Elsie suggested.

'With *much* love,' Sarah corrected. 'Put "with much love".'

Martin began carving.

'Shall we ever see Arnold again?' Elsie asked.
'Don't be silly, you know he's dead,' said Sarah.
'Yes, but I mean in Heaven.'
'Oh, in Heaven. Yes, I expect so.'
'Will Arnold meet our mum in Heaven?'
'Yes, of course.'
'How will they know each other?'
'They just *will*. Heaven's like that,' said Sarah.